PUFFIN BOOKS

Desperado Darlings

Here's what people said about *Little Darlings* and *Bad, Bad Darlings*:

'Every now and again, a children's book comes along that is completely different. *Little Darlings* is one of those' – *Sunday Times*

'Insanely funny about the appalling ways rich kids are brought up, this spunky British trio knock the Lemony Snicket siblings into a cocked hat' – *The Times*

'We've had this in the house for months and it has become dog-eared' – *Guardian*

'*Little Darlings* is an excellent book. Once you pick it up it's like an invisible padlock is fitted to you so you can't get away!' – Rhys, aged 11

And about *The Return of Death Eric*:

'. . . has the kind of knowing wit and cultural allusiveness that makes *The Simpsons* so funny. This is a smart, satirical, surprising read-aloud treat for all the family' – *Sunday Times*

'Hilarious children's *Spinal Tap*-style tale' *Sun*

More brilliant books by Sam Llewellyn

Little Darlings
Bad, Bad Darlings
The Return of Death Eric

Pig in the Middle
The Rope School
Pegleg

Desperado Darlings

Sam Llewellyn

Illustrated by David Roberts

PUFFIN

PUFFIN BOOKS

Published by the Penguin Group
Penguin Books Ltd, 80 Strand, London WC2R ORL, England
Penguin Group (USA) Inc., 375 Hudson Street, New York, New York 10014, USA
Penguin Group (Canada), 90 Eglinton Avenue East, Suite 700, Toronto, Ontario, Canada M4P 2Y3
(a division of Pearson Penguin Canada Inc.)
Penguin Ireland, 25 St Stephen's Green, Dublin 2, Ireland (a division of Penguin Books Ltd)
Penguin Group (Australia), 250 Camberwell Road, Camberwell, Victoria 3124, Australia
(a division of Pearson Australia Group Pty Ltd)
Penguin Books India Pvt Ltd, 11 Community Centre, Panchsheel Park, New Delhi – 110 017, India
Penguin Group (NZ), cnr Airborne and Rosedale Roads, Albany, Auckland 1310, New Zealand
(a division of Pearson New Zealand Ltd)
Penguin Books (South Africa) (Pty) Ltd, 24 Sturdee Avenue, Rosebank, Johannesburg 2196, South Africa

Penguin Books Ltd, Registered Offices: 80 Strand, London WC2R ORL, England

www.penguin.com

First published 2006
1

Set in Baskerville MT
Typeset by Palimpsest Book Production Limited, Polmont, Stirlingshire
Made and printed in England by Clays Ltd, St Ives plc

British Library Cataloguing in Publication Data
A CIP catalogue record for this book is available from the British Library

ISBN-10: 0-141-31981-x
ISBN-13: 978-0-141-31981-0

For Don Martín

Desperado Darlings
Meet the family. And some other people.

Daisy Darling
Age: $12^{7}/_{8}$
Likes: blood-red nail varnish, things working out just exactly precisely right
Dislikes: nannies, dictators, spoiltness in all its forms

Cassian Darling
Age: 11.521
Looks: from behind film of engine oil
Likes: explosions, coal bunkers, machinery in all its forms
Dislikes: cheap spanners, displays of emotion, cucumber

Primrose Darling
Age: $10^{2}/_{3}$
Likes: cooking with little-known and horrifying ingredients
Looks: small, pinkish, safe as milk
Is: dangerous as a truckload of high explosive cobras

The Captain
Age: would not even consider answering this question
Likes: pencil skirts, really delightful shoes, playing the lowdown blues
Dislikes: would not even consider answering this question

Papa Darling
Occupation: ex-tycoon and sanitary comptroller. All right, lower-deck lav cleaner
Likes: having supreme power and lovely briefcases
Dislikes: reality

Pete Fryer, aka Nanny Petronella
Occupation: nanny, burglar, all-round good egg
Likes: sparklers, wickedness of the nicer type, burgling songs
Weakness: the Captain in all her elegance and fragrancy. Sigh

HRH Crown Prince Beowulf of Iceland (deposed)
Occupation: Chief Engineer and lunatic
Loves: his teddy bear, the Royal Edward
Hates: EVERYVUN. EVERYVUN. EVERYVUN. OR MAYBE NOT

The Great One
Who?
Wait and seeeeeeeeeeeeeeeeeeece

Prologue

Tramp, went Nanny Dangerfield's brogues on the concrete quay. *Tramp, tramp.*

Nanny Dangerfield was taking a walk by the seaside. It was not a pretty seaside, but then Nanny Dangerfield was not a pretty nanny. Counting from south to north, Nanny Dangerfield wore steel-toecapped black brogues, thick cotton stockings, a heavyweight gingham dress with frills at sleeves and collar, and a brown bowler hat, its crown reinforced against flung toys and brickbats. Her forearms, bare in the balmy air, were mighty even for a nanny. Her granite jaw bristled with dark whiskers. Behind her low forehead, her mind was dark too.

The waterfront of Ciudad Olvidada was not, as I say, an attractive one. All right, the Caribbean Sea lapped against it. But what it was lapping against was not sand –

tramp, went the brogues –

but concrete. Grey, oil-splattered concrete with bits of rusty iron sticking out of it. Instead of seashells –

tramp –

there were broken bottles smeared with seagull muck. And instead of whispering palm trees there were huge rusty cranes, one after another down the quay, with wind sighing in their latticework –

tramp, tramp, tramp –

and more seagulls sitting at the top of long white streaks of filth. The only good thing about it, thought Nanny Dangerfield –

tramp, tramp –

was that there were no children anywhere in sight. Some nannies said that children should be seen and not heard. As far as Nanny Dangerfield was concerned, not seen was better, unless of course they were behind bars of some kind –

tramp —

and even then they were sure to cause trouble unless watched. *Closely* watched.

Nanny Dangerfield stopped. She took three deep breaths, spotted a cleanish bit of concrete, spat on her hands, did twenty quick press-ups, and stood up again. Her breathing had not quickened. She was a nanny in superb physical condition.

She looked out to sea, dusting off her horny palms. Her heavy brows came together in a frown.

Nanny Dangerfield liked the sea to be tidy. Today, the sea was not tidy. Out there on the glittering blue lay a sleek white ship. *The* ship. The one the Great One was Calling, which was Nanny Dangerfield's Task for Today. Nanny Dangerfield decided to stroll down to the end of the wharf and give the ship a hard stare and see if she could break its windows or melt it or at least add her little bit to the Call. Then she would climb into the rowing boat at the end of the quay and go and get that ship, as per the Great One's orders.

Tramp, tramp, tramp, went her brogues, accelerating.

Nanny Dangerfield came to the end of the quay. She scowled a bit, concentrating her mind on the ship. *Hubble, bubble,* went her teaspoonful of brain, boiling a little. No windows broke. Nothing melted. The ship stayed put. She turned to look for the rowing boat.

Halfway through the turn, something caught her eye.

It was a sort of platform attached to the cable of a crane. The platform had little railings round its sides, to prevent whatever it was that the crane was meant to lift from rolling off the sides and into the sea. In the middle of the platform something was sitting.

Nanny Dangerfield's great hands clenched into great fists, and her eyes became hot, thin slits.

Tramp.

The thing on the platform was a doll. It was made of ancient rags. On its head was a crude bowler hat made of brown cardboard. On its feet were black shoes. It was wearing a ragged gingham dress, with paper frills at collar and sleeves. Round its neck was a piece of paper.

It was meant to be a nanny.

Tramp, tramp.

Nanny Dangerfield stepped on to the platform and bent over the paper. Her thick lips moved as she spelled out the words.

ALL NANYS AR POO, said the words.

Nanny Dangerfield grunted with rage. Bad, *bad* people had been at work. They had insulted the Uniform. Somewhere inside, though, Nanny Dangerfield felt a trace of respect. They were clever little people. They could write, even quite long words like NANY.

Nanny Dangerfield straightened up, the doll in her hand, crumpling the paper with the bad words on it. Her nanny senses were alert. She could have sworn she had heard something go *clink*.

Suddenly she became aware that she was in a foolishly non-nanny position. She was on a platform under a crane, and her guard was down.

A whistle blew.

The platform under her feet leaped suddenly upward. This was because high overhead, the crane boom had started to move, and the crane cable had jerked taut, and the platform on its end had leaped off the quay and was whizzing in a great arc outwards, with Nanny Dangerfield still on it. Nanny Dangerfield felt her hat coming off. She let go of the rail to clamp the bowler to her head. At the exact moment she raised her hand, the platform reached the end of its travel. It stopped with a jerk.

Nanny Dangerfield went straight on.

A cloud of gulls burst from cranes and gantries. Out of the cloud soared the stocky figure in the nanny uniform, one hand on her hat, the other by her side, heading out to sea at an altitude of 211 metres and a speed of 309 kilometres per hour. Above the racket the gulls were making was another racket. It sounded like tiny cheers.

Naughty, *naughty* children, thought Nanny Dangerfield, whooshing grimly towards the glittering horizon.

It was the usual bright tropical morning on the absolutely fabulous ship *Kleptomanic II*. The Darling children were doing the usual morning things.

Under an awning on the bridge, Daisy Darling, the eldest, was playing chess with a very small burglar called Nosey Clanger.

In the Grand Saloon, Cassian Darling, the middle one, was inside a grand piano which had gone wrong. Cassian knew nothing about pianos. But he loved his mother, the Captain of the *Kleptomanic*.

And the Captain loved playing the piano. In Cassian's view pianos were only machines, and machines were what Cassian was very, very good at, so there he was, inside the piano, mending it.

In the ship's enormous galley, Primrose Darling, the youngest, was helping Chef. Or rather Chef was helping her construct a cheese and blackcurrant-jam sorbet with mint trim. Primrose was an inspired cook. Chef had started cooking 20 years and 100 kilos ago, and he recognized genius when he saw it.

On the bridge, the Captain, cool in a taupe linen sheath dress, was allowing herself to look forward to a really lovely cocktail. Pete Fryer, burglar and friend of the Darlings, was darning his striped jersey and casting sideways glances of an adoring nature at the Captain. The helmsman was steering, and elsewhere in the ship the oilers were oiling, and Papa Darling, father of the Darling children, was scrubbing the floor of number three lower-deck lav and hoping that someone would promote him to a better job without delay. Shipboard life, in fact, was plumb normal.

But not for long.

Wait for it.

Here we go.

The ship's clock struck eleven.

Cassian Darling climbed out of the piano and headed for the bridge. Primrose Darling shook hands with Chef, shrugged out of her apron and headed for the bridge. Daisy Darling, of course, was already on the bridge.

The Captain was peering out to sea, shading her eyes against the sun with a long, elegant hand. 'Goodness,' she said. 'What was *that*?'

Daisy Darling followed the Captain's wise and kindly gaze, giving Nosey Clanger a chance to steal a couple of her pawns. Primrose's eyes followed her sister's.

'The engines have stopped,' said Cassian. 'Both of them.'

'This is no time to be gibbering about engines,' said Daisy. 'Look!' She pointed at the tiny figure streaking across the sky.

Cassian looked. Under its usual film of black oil, his face seemed worried. 'A flying nanny,' he said. 'Yeah, sure. Look, I'd better run down and see if everything is all right.'

'Engines, engines, *engines*!' said Daisy, sighing.

So there they were, at the beginning of the story: the Darling family; the *Kleptomanic II*, white and beautiful on the tropic blue; the land, the white, Spanish-looking buildings of the port with the green, tropical mountains of . . .

'What's this place?' said Daisy.

'Nananagua, it says here,' said the Captain, waving an elegant hand at the chart.

. . . Nananagua, rising into dark and thundery clouds in the inland distance. And over it all, outlined against the sky, one hand on bowler hat, the other punched out ahead in the Superman position, a flying nanny.

'Down she comes,' said Primrose.

Down she came. Daisy's chessmen rocked in the nanny's slipstream as she howled over the bridge and augered into the sea alongside with a splash like a bomb bursting.

The Captain raised a perfect eyebrow and stifled a yawn. She said, 'I suppose we had better lower a boat.'

'Perhaps,' said Daisy, but there was doubt in her voice.

For in the patch of turbulent water where the Flying Nanny had landed, a patch of greater turbulence had erupted. It turned into a massive head, on to which two hands crammed a bowler hat. Sun glittered in black eyes as the head looked around. The eyes settled on the ship. Muscular arms surfaced. The Flying Nanny started towards the *Kleptomanic* at a powerful crawl.

'Oops,' said Primrose.

For behind the Flying Nanny two large black fins were cutting through the water. Fins of this kind are almost always attached to sharks, except when they are attached to killer whales, and killer whales are rare in the Caribbean.

'She's quite a swimmer,' said Daisy.

The nanny in the water was indeed doing well. For about 50 metres, the positions were as follows: nanny, 5 metres of water, shark, shark. But sharks are born to swim, and nannies are not.

'They're catching up,' said Daisy grimly.

'C'*mon*, sharks,' said Primrose. The Darling children had been brought up by seventeen nannies one after the other, and old habits die hard.

The nanny was getting closer to the ship. The black fins were getting closer to the nanny. The black fins were getting closer to the nanny faster than the nanny was getting closer to the ship.

'Perhaps this would be a good moment to turn away and look at something pleasant,' said Daisy.

'I do so agree,' said the Captain.

But for once in her life she was wrong.

The fins were now one and a half metres behind the bowler hat. The ghastly jaws were open, the fearsome teeth ready for action, the black brogues waggling temptingly within range.

'Eek,' said Daisy.

'Hey!' said Primrose.

For the bowler hat had stopped. The fins rushed on. The nanny turned, lifted two hefty fists and whacked them down on something in the water. Then she did it again. The fins turned floppy. They milled around uselessly, then wobbled off towards the horizon, bumping into each other from time to time.

'Cor,' said Primrose.

'Nosey!' cried the Captain.

'Yeff,' said Daisy's tiny and heavily tattooed chess opponent, getting up from the board, where he had finished stealing pawns and was furtively rearranging the pieces into a pattern that would let him checkmate in three moves.

'Normally at sea one says "Aye, aye",' said the Captain kindly. 'Pop a rope ladder over the side, there's a dear.'

'And watch yourself,' said Daisy.

'Huh,' said Nosey. He had really wanted to win at chess, but Duty was Duty. He clenched his aniseed-ball-sized fists and trotted off.

The telephone rang. 'Hello?' murmured the Captain.

Daisy and Primrose watched her. She said, 'Do what you can,' and put the phone down.

'Well?' said Daisy.

'That was Cassian. A little trouble with the Chief Engineer.'

Wait a minute. What, you will be asking yourself, is this all about? Flying nannies? Ships carrying people called Darling?

All right, all right.

The Darling children used to live in a large house with their rich Papa and his second wife, Mrs Darling II. Their life was once full of money but empty of love, run by nannies of the fiercest kind. After they had mentally and physically wrecked seventeen nannies, the Darling children had become tough and clever. So when the burglar Pete Fryer turned up at their house disguised as a nanny, they had followed him back to the burglars' lair or den, where they found that the burglars were lovely people, or anyway much nicer than anyone at home.

This lair or den was actually an ocean liner called the *Kleptomanic*. Once Cassian had got it working with the help of the mad Chief Engineer, the *Kleptomanic* had gone to sea. At this point the Captain had turned out to be the Darlings' long-lost mother. The ship had paused to rescue Papa Darling from a desert island and put him to work in the lavs where he would learn humility. Then the Darlings and their burglarious crew had sailed west to Neverglade, home of millionaires. Here the *Kleptomanic* bumped into an island and sank, so the Darlings and their burglar friends were forced to swipe a luxury yacht, which they had rechristened the *Kleptomanic II*. The only blot on the horizon was the Chief Engineer. Any sailor will tell you that the Chief Engineer is usually a blot on the horizon. On the *Kleptomanic II*, there was frankly more blot than horizon.

Clear? Good. Where were we?

Here.

Once, the Chief Engineer had been the heir to the throne of Iceland. Then he had been thrown out by a revolution. His real name was Chief Engineer Crown Prince Beowulf of Iceland (deposed), B.Eng. Reykjavik. Like all Chief Engineers, he was a creature of powerful emotions. Like all royals, he had so many screws loose that when he shook his head it sounded like a toolbox. And like many of his fellow country-men, he was very, very keen on codfish and volcanoes, sometimes to the point where they interfered with his work.

'What is it this time?' said Daisy, folding her lips, for she did not altogether approve of codfish or, for that matter, volcanoes.

'He has read an atlas in the ship's library. This one,' said the Captain, holding up the mighty and ancient volume. 'Apparently Nananagua is famous for its volcano, which is called El Grande. He wishes to stop here and have a look at it. Nananagua is by all accounts a hellhole. It contains nothing worth burgling and should be avoided at all costs, it says here. Which is why I wish to pass it and go on to Palmbeachia, which is full of millionaires and delicious shrimps. Oh, dear,' said the Captain. 'Perhaps he will calm down.'

'Perhaps,' said Daisy and Primrose, without much hope, for they knew the Chief well.

'And here comes the Flying Nanny,' said the Captain, glad of a chance to change the subject.

They looked over the side. A rope ladder dangled in the water. The nanny started to swarm up it.

With a grunt and a creak of ropes she arrived on deck. She stood glowering about her, huge and dripping.

'Oooooo *naughty*!' she hissed, obviously put out by her recent flight. Then her eyes settled on Primrose.

Primrose took a paper bag out of her pocket. 'Butterscotch, Nana?' she said, with a sweet smile.

'No, ta,' said the nanny. She blinked. Primrose thought she looked as if she was listening to something far away. 'But,' said the Flying Nanny, 'this is ever such a nice ship. Could I see round?'

'Obviously,' said Primrose, reluctantly, for she was suspicious of nannies, but all sailors must offer hospitality to the rescued swimmer. 'Luggage!' She beckoned over a giant stoker with a handle growing out of the back of his head. 'Will you give Nana the Grand Tour?'

'Hur, hur,' said Luggage, looking at his enormous feet and going red.

'Oo,' said Nanny Dangerfield.

Primrose watched the two gigantic people lumber off. Unless she was much mistaken, they fancied each other.

Yuk.

*

Cassian was not absolutely sure about the engine room of the *Kleptomanic II*. The engine rooms he really liked were filthy warrens of iron and coal and jets of steam. The *Kleptomanic II*'s was painted white. The brass pipes of the twin engines were polished to a high shine, and the great propeller shafts turned in their trenches with a low, soothing drone. Well, thought Cassian, the main thing was that it worked.

Normally.

Today, things were not normal. The serried valves were silent, the shafts motionless. The only sound as Cassian walked between the engines were the pad of his engineer's boots and the sound of a pencil rolling to and fro, to and fro on a desk as the waves ran under the ship.

In the corner of the engine room was a glass hut. Cut-out paper crowns were stuck to the windows and the curtains were drawn. Cassian tapped on the door. 'Well?' he said.

'Vell vot?' said a voice.

'We've got to start the engines,' said Cassian.

'Vy?'

'Because they're stopped.'

'Ja. I stopped 'em.'

Cassian understood engines. People were different.

They had an odd bendy way of thinking that Cassian did not understand and did not want to. The Chief thought in the bendiest way Cassian had ever come across. 'Why?' he said.

'LA LA LA LA CAN'T HEAR YOU,' howled the Chief. A shutter flew aside. Behind it was the familiar pear-shaped face with spiked helmet above and dribble-soaked teddy bear buttoned into the tunic below.

'Hur, hur,' said a voice at Cassian's side.

Turning, he saw Giant Luggage and a gigantic nanny with a brown bowler hat and hairy forearms.

'MY LIFE HAS NO MEANINK!' cried the Chief.

'Wha?'

'THEY SAY, HERE ARE WOLCANOES, THEN THEY TAKE THEM AVAY!'

'Bu–'

'I VANT A WOLCANO!' cried the Chief.

'Perhaps you will get one,' said the nanny.

'VOOPEE!' cried the Chief, eyes whirling.

Cassian sighed. 'Nice as this is,' he said to the nanny, 'I am going to have to get the ship going. So would you excuse me?'

'Oo,' grated Nanny Dangerfield. 'There's a clever

little man then. Could you drop me ashore?'

Cassian did not like nannies in general and this one in particular. 'Spose,' he said. 'Stand aside there.' He took off his uniform cap and substituted an oily baseball hat. 'We will be moving in ten minutes.' Assisted by Luggage, he began the engine-starting procedures, while the Flying Nanny stood by the Chief's shutter. She seemed to be murmuring something. It sounded to Cassian to contain the words Great One and Kodsfjord. But he was not listening, being busy.

At minute nine, the procedures were complete. 'All clear?' Cassian said to Luggage.

'Hur, hur,' said Luggage, casting an admiring glance at the nanny, who cast one back.

'Starting,' said Cassian. His hand went to the *Kleptomanic*'s great golden key and turned it. Air hissed. Pistons turned. Fuel caught and exploded. The discreet thrum of great engines rose through the *Kleptomanic*'s hull. Her white nose turned towards the shore.

Forty-seven seconds later, several things were going on. The Chief was still in his hut, probably sulking. The burglars were having lunch in the dining saloon. Cassian was in the control room, biting into a cheese and tomato sandwich and monitoring the control panels. High on the bridge Lars Chance, the Sailing Master, stood at the wheel, looking out of the window.

The harbour of Ciudad Olvidada lay spread in front of the ship's bow. It was an unpleasant-looking stretch of water, coated with oily scum. Lars had been the *Kleptomanic II*'s Captain before the Darlings had stolen and renamed the ship. Obviously, he loved and respected the Captain. He loved the food that Primrose and the Chef produced. He quite liked the burglars for their rough good humour. But most of all, he loved the *Kleptomanic*.

Lars squinted under the shining peak of his immaculate cap. Straight ahead was a concrete quay. The sort of place where you could drop off a dangerous nanny, then head out to sea. His hand went to the engine-room telegraph. Time to slow down, ready for the delicate positioning of his beloved alongside the quay.

Nanny Dangerfield was thinking. That man with the tattoos on his face and the handle on the back of his head.

Rrrrr, thought Nanny Dangerfield.

Giant Luggage was thinking too. Nanny Dangerfield. Big and strong.

Phwoar.

But Nanny Dangerfield was thinking something else. She was thinking that the day had started badly, but was ending well. The Great One was going to be very, very pleased.

When Lars Chance hauled the engine-room telegraph lever back, a bell rang and a pointer on the dial in the control room went to STOP ENGINES. Cassian reached out to pull the lever that stopped the engines.

He only got halfway.

There was a howl. Two huge white spiders hurtled across the control room and grabbed his arm. Not spiders, he realized. Hands. Attached to the arms of Chief Engineer Crown Prince Beowulf of Iceland (deposed). The hands wrenched Cassian off his chair and slammed the lever to FULL AHEAD. Over the racket of the engines, someone seemed to be shrieking.

'Wha?' said Cassian.

'VANTINK TO GO ASHORE!' cried the

Chief, spraying dribble. 'VANTINK TO SEE ZIS COUNTRY, ZO WOLKANIC! LOOK! I AM SITTING ON ZE LEVER!'

'– slow down,' said Cassian.

'VOT?' cried the Chief, who was indeed sitting on the lever, his eyes whirling in separate directions.

'Nothing,' said Cassian. The only person who could move the Chief when he was Off On One was Giant Luggage, and Giant Luggage had left the engine room. Meanwhile, the *Kleptomanic II* was hurtling ahead at full speed instead of stopping. Sooner or later, there was going to be a really enormous crash.

'STOPPP!' bellowed Lars Chance into the telephone. The ship was thundering down the narrow channel towards the smelly quay. There was no room to turn round. All Lars could do was cling to the telephone with one hand and the wheel with the other and grit his teeth and hope for the best. Oh, and shout, 'NOOOOOOOO!'

Cassian leaned forward. He twitched the teddy bear out of the Chief's tunic, hauled a monkey wrench out of his pocket, put the bear on the steel deck and held the wrench above its head. 'Stop,' he said. 'Or the bear gets it.'

The Chief's eyes popped open, crossed, uncrossed. 'MEIN EDVARD!' he howled. 'YOU PROMISED NEVER AGAIN!'

'Oops!' said Cassian, tossing the bear out of the control-room door.

The Chief went after the bed animal. Cassian locked the door and hauled the lever back to FULL ASTERN.

This is the ship equivalent of jamming the brakes on.

Too late.

Once, Papa Darling had been Chief Executive of Darling Gigantic, a major player in the concreting-over-nature-reserves field. Nowadays he was Sanitary Comptroller or chief lavatory cleaner on the *Kleptomanic II*. The Captain had said he was free to work his way up. The future, she had said, was in his hands.

What was actually in his hands at this precise moment was a mop and a bucket. Papa Darling did not like it. But he was deep down in the front end of the ship, and he could see no way out.

Gagging slightly, he opened the next cubicle door and swung his bucket inside.

As the bucket hit the floor, the world went mad. There was a roar of engines and a shocking crash. Papa Darling was hurled in the cubicle. He came up spluttering into complete darkness.

Into not quite complete darkness.

Where once there had been the steel plating of the ship's hull there was now a ragged gash through which daylight filtered. Beyond the gash was concrete.

Papa Darling was looking at a hole in the ship's side.

To most of the crew of the *Kleptomanic*, it would have looked like a disaster.

Not to Papa Darling.

To Papa Darling, it looked like a career development opportunity.

The Chief Engineer picked himself up from the floor. He scowled, his great lower lip swinging. All he wanted was a little volcano time. And all he got were crashing ships. 'Edvard,' he murmured, drooling on his teddy. Well, he would lock himself in and count his cousins in his head.

He locked himself in. He began the count at King Adolphus of Aaarr. He had got as far as Grand Elector Azog of Mormia the Lesser when he stopped.

Someone was talking in his head.

This was not unusual for a royal person. But this was a fairly new voice. He had been hearing it for a couple of days. Now it was even louder than the grinding of his teeth.

Come to meeeeee, it seemed to be calling, sweet as a correctly lubricated turbocharger. *I understaaaaaand.* Then there were some other instructions.

Suddenly the Chief Engineer remembered the things the big nanny had told him earlier. Things about the Great One. And Kodsfjord. He must Heed the Call. Oh yessss . . .

The Chief Engineer blinked. Then he stood up. He buttoned the Royal Edward more firmly into his tunic. He packed a summer-weight crown and a set of spanners. He wrote a note. He walked towards the iron stairs leading upward.

Anyone looking at him would have found his face expressionless, his eyes glazed. But everyone who might have seen him was piled up in a great ball of food and humanity against the front wall of the dining saloon, except Cassian, who was not looking. So nobody got a chance.

I understaaaaaaaand, crooned the new voice in his head.

'Ja, OK, comink, Great Vun,' said the Chief.

He walked down the gangplank, climbed into the long black limo that whispered up alongside him, and was gone.

2

The *Kleptomanic II* lay with her nose embedded in the concrete quay. Flies buzzed over dead fish. Skinny dogs loped to and fro in the hot streets of Ciudad Olvidada. The library of the *Kleptomanic*, where the Darlings were having a quick meeting, was an oasis of air-conditioned comfort.

'Ahem,' said Daisy, opening the *Greasy Planet Guide to the South*. '"Nananagua. Previously known as the Costa Pestifera or Smelly Coast. Capital, Ciudad Olvidada, which means Forgotten City. Famed for its mountains, which include several active volcanoes, and its revolutions, which are surprisingly frequent."'

The children watched a dead pig float past the window. Daisy put the guidebook tidily back on the shelf and said, 'Well, we'll just have to make the best of it for a few days until the ship gets mended. I'm going on deck.'

Outside, the air smelt like a fridge after a four-day power cut. The sun glared off the concrete.

'Stone me,' said Primrose.

The rail was lined with burglars. The gangway was down. At the entrance to the gangway stood Giant Luggage. His head hung forward on his massive chest. From time to time he shook it and said, 'Hur, hur,' in a small, hopeless voice.

'What is it?' said Daisy.

'Hur,' he said, and pointed down the gangway.

'Goodness,' said Daisy.

The Flying Nanny was marching down it. Its shoreward end was entirely blocked by small men in uniform. The crowd of uniforms parted before the nanny, revealing three more nannies who had been standing behind it. They wore pale-green gingham dresses, heavy black brogues and brown bowler hats. Their chins were hairy, and their little eyes glinted with cunning. The men in uniform cast nervous glances at them.

Luggage waved at the Flying Nanny. The Flying Nanny waved back.

'Anyone for a run ashore?' said Daisy.

'It's not that easy,' said Pete's voice behind her.

'Don't be silly,' said Daisy, and marched down the gangway. 'Good afternoon, good afternoon!' she cried in a high, bracing voice. 'So this is Nananagua! How lovely!'

'Get back from the edge!' cried the nannies as one nanny.

'Have you got permission?' cried a solo nanny.

'Get a lifejacket!' cried another.

'Well!' said Daisy, smiling with a kindness she most certainly did not feel. 'What a lot of bossiness!'

'Children should be seen and not heard!' said yet another nanny.

'Go to your room!' cried the first.

And before Daisy could draw breath to smile again, two nannies had picked her up, one by each arm, and carted her back on to the *Kleptomanic*, her feet pedalling the air.

'Probably best to stay on board,' said the Captain, after she had taken her extremely indignant daughter to the bridge. 'Let us do our repairs and get out of here.'

But it was not going to be as easy as that.

Wait for it.

The city of Ciudad Olvidada drowsed under its mountains. Even the many fleas had found little wedges of shade where they lay snoring in a small, high chorus. Only on the *Kleptomanic II* was there life and movement. An elite squad of safecrackers was dangling over the side, welding the ship's wrecked metal plates. In a surprisingly short time, the *Kleptomanic* stopped looking like a crash scene and started looking like the elegant superyacht she really was.

'Marvellous!' cried the Captain, as she did her rounds with Pete Fryer that evening.

'Lower deck present and sober,' said Lower Deck Dave, Captain of the Lower Deck, standing to attention in front of a door and saluting.

'Fabulous!' cried the Captain.

But Pete Fryer was frowning. 'Move one step to your left,' he said. 'Please.'

Lower Deck Dave turned pale. He took the step. He had been standing in front of a door. On the door was written the word TOILET. Over the word TOILET hung a sign that said OUT OF ORDER.

'Open up,' said Pete.

'Nggg,' said Dave.

The Captain sighed. 'How much did he pay you?' she said.

'Nuffink,' said Dave.

'What did he promise you, then? Wealth? Power? Fame?'

'It's a fair cop,' said Dave. 'All of 'em. Then he done a runner.'

'Sigh,' said the Captain, and pushed open the door.

'??!' cried everyone, reeling away from the truly ghastly stench that rolled into the corridor –

Sorry, reader. What, you will be asking yourself, is he on about? OK, OK.

You will remember that Papa Darling, father of Daisy, Cassian and Primrose, was Sanitary Comptroller of the *Kleptomanic*. Not a dignified job, and not at all what he was used to. Well, now he had escaped and paid Lower Deck Dave to cover up for him.

'This time,' said the Captain, 'I think we really, really must leave Papa behind.'

'You sure?' said Pete Fryer, scarcely able to keep the excitement out of his voice, for he loved the Captain silently but dearly, and Papa Darling was a constant obstacle to his happiness. 'Oh, hello, Cassian.'

'Darling boy!' cried the Captain. 'You have missed the most *tragic* scene! Now then, do go and tell the Chief to start engines and off we go!'

'Not possible,' said Cassian. His face had a stunned look, as if someone had used it to hit a baseball a long distance.

'Come on,' said the Captain. 'Off we go.'

Cassian shook his head. A few nuts and bolts fell out of his hair. 'We can't,' he said.

'But of *course* we can!'

'No,' he said. 'He's not there. I found this.' He handed over a piece of paper.

It was a note. The words were written in green ink, apparently by someone using both hands. I RESINE, it said. I EM ON DER BEACH VERE I AM APPREESIATED AND THERE IS GOOD WOLKANO. FAREVELL.

'Stone me,' said Pete.

'And he's taken the key,' said Cassian.

'The key?'

'The key to the ship. The only one of its kind in the universe. Irreplaceable.'

'What can we *do*?' said the Captain.

'Make a plan,' said Daisy firmly.

And up they all trooped to the bridge.

The Captain sat down in one of the chintz armchairs in the wheelhouse. 'So we are stuck,' she said. 'And our Sanitary Comptroller has done a runner, importance rating two –'

'Three,' said Daisy, loyally.

'– OK, three out of ten. And the Chief Engineer has done a runner, ten –'

'– eleven,' said Cassian, judiciously.

'– OK, eleven out of ten.'

'Plus he may have been kidnapped, not done a runner,' said Primrose.

'Not kidnapped,' said Cassian. 'Sort of lured, I think.'

Eight eyes swivelled to cover him. 'Lured?' said Daisy.

'That Flying Nanny was whispering in his ear,' said Cassian.

'Whispering what?'

'Kodsfjord, she said. And Great One. I think

Kodsfjord was where he lived as a child. Dunno about Great Ones, though. Anyway, it was after she talked to him that he started to act weird.'

'He always acts weird.'

'Weirder than usual.'

'Ah.' There was a silence.

Then the Captain said, 'Perhaps one of those guard people would like a cup of tea.'

'And a chat?' said Daisy.

'Leave it to me,' said Pete. He got up and left the bridge. The Darlings heard his voice shout 'Anyone speak English?' followed by some confused sounds of struggle. Then he was back, holding a small man with a moustache by the scruff of the neck. 'This,' said Pete, 'is Sergeant Boracico –'

'Fantastico,' corrected the Sergeant, his eyes flicking nervously round the wheelhouse. He had never seen a ship's wheel with frills on before.

'So,' said Daisy, 'we have a missing person.'

'Two,' said Cassian.

'Oh yes. Sergeant Amazingo, we are looking for our Chief Engineer. A nanny came on board and whispered something about a Great One in his ear. And now he has gone. Will you help us find him . . . are you all right?'

For Sergeant Fantastico had gone pale and his knees were knocking.

Primrose gave him a drink of water. 'Spit it out,' she said. She wiped her sandals. 'Not the water, silly.'

'Tell us,' said the Captain, oozing charm in all directions.

'So we will be warned,' said Daisy cleverly. 'And very afraid, obviously.'

'Warned,' said the Sergeant. 'Yes. Well. The Nana who came on board was Nanny Dangerfield. Nanny Dangerfield is one of the nannies who . . .' His voice trailed away. The knocking of his knees sounded like a coconut rolling down stone steps.

'Yes?' said the Captain.

'She works for the Great One,' said the Sergeant, speaking quickly, as if he wanted to get this over with. 'The Great One controls the Nanas, who make sure everyone is safe and behaves well. The Nanas control us, the police, that is. And we control the people. We are guarding the ship in case our people try to creep on board and flee our so lovely country. Can I go now?'

'You are the police,' said Daisy. 'Policemen help members of the public find missing persons.'

'In Nananagua? In your dreams,' said Sergeant Fantastico. A subtle police twist took him out of Pete's hands, and he bolted down the gangway.

'Well!' said Daisy, shocked. 'So are we to assume that the Chief has gone off to look for this Great One?'

The Captain shrugged. 'Quite possibly.'

'But why?'

'We'll just have to find out,' said Primrose.

The Captain said, 'I really don't think this is a suitable place for you to go ashore.'

'Are you saying,' said Primrose, 'that we should be more nervous about this place than this place should be of *us*?'

'Perish the thought!' cried the Captain.

'Wait a minute, children,' said noble Pete Fryer. 'This is a hot spot. So it is me that is going to go and look for this here Great One and the Chief et cetera.'

'And Papa.'

'Him too. To avoid trouble I shall put on nanny disguise. They seem to fear nannies round these parts,' said Pete. 'Obviously I shall go after nightfall.'

Six cold eyes glared at Pete. The little Darlings did not like to be left behind. Then Daisy reminded herself that basically they did all love Pete. She gave him her sweetest (but not sincerest) smile. 'Anything you say,' she said. 'Come, fellow children.'

The Darlings went straight to their suite and gathered in the drawing room, which had white leather sofas and a glass coffee table.

'Well?' said Primrose, pouring heaped glasses of Fruit Surprise all round.

Daisy was already in the clothes cupboard, hauling out brogues, bowler hats and greenish dresses. Five minutes later, a small but determined nanny stood before Cassian and Primrose.

'Very convincing,' said Cassian, with a slight shudder. 'What is your exact plan?'

'I'm going to wait for Pete to go ashore and follow him stealthily. If I'm not back in two hours, send help.'

'Aye, aye, Daise,' said Cassian and Primrose admiringly.

As the last red chip of the sun sank between two scruffy palm trees, the familiar stocky figure of Pete Fryer, alias Nanny Petronella, beetled down the gangway. Daisy heard the clump of brogues and saw the glint of the PRESENT FROM EASTBOURNE brooch. She heard the voice order aside the policemen at the gangway's foot. She heard the policemen's nervous voices saying, 'Pass, Nana.'

'My turn,' said Daisy to herself. She folded her lips. Then she marched down the gangway until she could smell the hair oil on the policemen. She had already started her Nanny Incantation. 'Oo just *wait* till I catch Nanny Tooth,' she said in a high, mad croon. 'She'll forget her own head next – Hello boys,' she said, looking up at the half-circle of moustaches and peaked caps blocking her off from the quay. 'I am Nanny Fang, Nanny Tooth's mate or oppo, and do you know what, she has forgotten the nice red flannel for wrapping up little Bertoletta, such a weak chest, that's Lady Wishwash's sister's husband's step–'

'Aiee!' cried a policeman, maddened with boredom. 'This one is only small! Shall we fleeng her in the sea?'

'No, no, let her pass, a Nana is a Nana and the Great One has eyes everywhere,' said another policeman, making a curse gesture. 'Fall in a hole, Nana.'

'Ssh! In case the Great One hears!'

'Aye.'

'Too right.'

The wall of bored policemen parted in front of Daisy. She began to walk briskly across the smelly concrete towards the city. Thanks to her nanny uniform, no one came near her.

Ahead of her the stocky figure of Pete Fryer rolled along, half burglar, half sailor, half nanny, larger than life. Daisy knew that if she caught Pete up, he would send her straight back to the ship. So she hung back as the quay gave way to a road between big sheds and the road narrowed into alleys between dirty white houses. The ground was sloping upward. Beyond the houses, she caught a glimpse of something that might have been a very grim palace or a fairly grim prison.

After a while, Pete passed a doorway from which fell shafts of light and the sound of guitars. He glanced furtively left and right. Then he hid his bowler hat on a ledge, tucked his nanny skirt into his nanny knickers, and popped in through the door.

Tch, thought Daisy. She crept up and peered through the window.

The place seemed to be a pub. A man in a big hat was playing the guitar in a corner, and the portrait of a pink-faced nanny hung on the wall next to a sign that said HAVING FUN? IS IT WISE? Pete was accepting a glass of something from a barman, winking and asking questions. Frankly he looked pretty odd. The nanny part of his clothes seemed to be making the barman nervous. A thin man with a long red nose, sitting two down the bar, edged away. What Daisy could see but Pete could not was that the man with the long red nose had gone to a payphone. A notice over the phone said STOP HIM? SHOP HIM! There was a number. The man with the long red nose dialled it.

Five minutes later Pete came back into the street, wiping his mouth with the back of his hand in a non-nannyish manner. He went into another bar, which had the same nanny picture on the wall next to a notice that said LAUGHING CAN BE HARMFUL TO YOUR HEALTH. When he came out of this one he was wiping his mouth again, and also singing a tune. His feet looked slightly over-cheerful as they moved over the cobbles. In one more pub's time, he would definitely be dancing a hornpipe.

Tch, thought Daisy.

Behind her a van door slammed. Hobnails sounded on cobblestones. Swiftly, she glided into a dark doorway. The hobnails charged past. She stepped back into the street.

Dearie dearie *me*, thought Daisy.

Ahead of her were three huge figures in skirts and bowler hats. They were nannies, gigantic ones. They were bearing down on the neat but now definitely dancing figure of Pete Fryer.

'Oh, the HIDDLYdee da deep a deepa deep dee,' cried Pete, leaping into the air and clashing his heels together.

One of the monster nannies reached out a hand and caught him by the scruff of the uniform, still in midair.

'Ooer,' said Pete. 'Wha?'

'Evening, Nanny,' said the giant.

'Evenin', Nanny,' said Pete, recovering his sangfroid or cool. 'Would you mind putting me down? Only it's draughty up here.'

'Password,' said the giant.

'Password?' said Pete.

Somewhere behind her, Daisy heard a faint *clink*.

Another van drew up. More brogues clashed on more cobbles. Daisy shrank into a new doorway. The street twinkled with sparks from the hobnails of reinforcement nannies.

'Oi,' said Pete.

'Shush, vermin,' said the arresting nanny in a huge, gravelly voice. 'Pretending to be a Nana is a big, big offence.'

'*Naughty,*' said another Nana.

Another of the nanny squad came back to meet the reinforcements. They met not three metres from Daisy's doorway. She caught a whiff like hot horses washed with strong soap. A harsh whisper said, 'Password?'

'Rockabye baby.'

'Pass, friend,' said the nanny.

'You have a prisoner?'

'A very, very naughty one. Singing, dancing, Impersonating a Nana. The Great One will be sooo pleased.'

'Off to the Caboose, then?'

'The Caboose it is.'

Clink, went something down the street.

The feet tramped on.

'Oi!' shouted Pete. 'Leggo!'

Daisy forced herself to close her ears to her friend's cries. She slid back through the shadows of Ciudad Olvidada towards the ship.

Again the *clink*. But this time she did not hear it.

Nor did she see the manhole cover in the street rise, nor the two eyes, large, brown and highly intelligent, that glowed faintly in the dark slot under the manhole cover, taking in the busy scene.

Clink. The cover settled back into its socket. The church clocks struck ten, one after the other. The streets became empty except for rats and other creatures of the night.

There were plenty of those in Ciudad Olvidada.

The Chief Engineer was in the limo. It was a nice limo, with a happy engine. The walls of the back bit were padded with crimson satin. There were windows, but he could not see out, because curtains with pink bunnies on were drawn across them, and besides, he was not interested in looking out of windows because he was sitting on a throne, and it was a long time since he had sat on a throne, particularly a comfy one like this, and he could look out of windows any time, but this sitting on thrones was the kind of enjoyment that needed to be concentrated on.

And among the many voices in his head, one voice crooned. *Welcome hoooooome, Your Royal Highness,* it went. *If I may make so bold as to address you thus.*

43

'You may!' cried the Chief Engineer. 'Yas, yas, Great One, you may!'

Excellent, said the crooning voice. *And now you are going to meeeet some people. Important people. But none so important as yooooooou!*

The Chief said nothing. He was too busy gnawing delightedly at the arm of his throne.

3

'*Pete?*' said the Captain. 'In *prison*? And put there by *nannies*?'

'I'm afraid so,' said Daisy. 'They're like normal nannies, but not like them. Much tougher.'

'You took such *risks*!' said the Captain.

'In the line of duty,' said Daisy. 'And now I am determined to find this Great One and give him a good talking-to. Lock up Pete, forsooth! Kidnap the Chief! The idea!'

'Wait!' cried the Captain.

'No time,' said Daisy. 'Goodness knows when they change that password, but you can bet it will be soon.'

The Captain sighed and passed her endless fingers over her noble brow. 'Have it your own way, then. You have destroyed, what, sixteen nannies?'

'Seventeen,' said Daisy, with quiet pride.

'Well,' said the Captain, 'go to this prison if you must.' Daisy saw the Captain's reflection in the wheelhouse window brush away what might have been a tear. 'And bring my Pete back safe. Now then. Off you go!'

Daisy saluted crisply and left the wheelhouse. Primrose was standing outside the door, dressed (Daisy was surprised to note) in full nanny gear.

'Let's go,' said Primrose.

'You?' said Daisy.

Primrose patted her satchel. 'I brought a picnic,' she said. 'Some of it's for us. And some of it isn't.'

'It is always nice to share,' said Daisy.

Off they trotted.

When they saw the uniforms, the policemen at the bottom of the gangway parted like rabbits in front of two tigers. The small nannies walked briskly into

Ciudad Olvidada through dark and smelly streets. There was a thin moon. By its light, Daisy could see the grim Caboose looming above the city. In one of its towers a light burned dim and yellow.

'Ten past ten, and all quiet,' said Primrose.

'I think,' said Daisy, 'that everyone is Tucked Up Nicely In Bed.'

They walked on.

'What was that?' said Primrose.

'What was what?'

'A sort of clink noise.'

'Didn't hear anything.'

They walked on some more.

The houses grew bigger and the smell grew worse. Suddenly they found themselves in a cobbled square. On the far side was a high wall made of large rocks covered in flaking white paint. In the wall was a grim gate. Over the gate was written THE CABOOSE — ABANDON HOPE ALL YE WHO ENTER HERE. There was a portcullis and a drawbridge. Higher up in the darkness there seemed to be various chutes. One had a notice that said DANGER — BOILING OIL — HOT. Another said CAUTION — MOLTEN LEAD — MAY CAUSE BURNING ALIVE. A third said CONTAINS LIVE SCORPIONS.

Even less welcoming than possible scorpions were two gigantic nannies standing at the end of the drawbridge. They were knitting. Daisy did not like the look of the needles. Too long, for one thing. Too sharp, for another.

She took a deep breath. 'Evening, Nanas!' she cried, striding towards the drawbridge.

The Nanas did not have the politeness to return her merry greeting. They merely shifted their grip on their knitting needles.

'Password,' said the one on the right.

'Rockabye baby.'

'Pass, friends,' said the one on the left.

'Have a mint?' said Primrose.

Both the guard nannies swivelled their eyes. They saw a small pink nanny with yellow hair, holding out a tin of peppermints.

'Extra strong,' said Primrose.

For nannies, the combination of total cleanness and agonizing painfulness makes Extra Strong Mints hard to resist. Two crane-hook hands came down and grabbed. Two granite jaws said, '*Thenk* you,' and crunched. Two huge sets of lungs said, 'Woo.'

'What we would really *love*,' said Daisy, 'is to know

how we can get to visit the nanny who was taken here earlier for not knowing the password.'

One of the guard nannies' lips moved to say, 'You are under arrest.' The words that actually came out, weirdly twisted, were, 'Through the door, down the steps, along the tunnel, through the water, third on the right, cell five, can't miss it. Key's on the nail.'

'Thank you so much,' said Daisy.

'Why don't you take a long walk off a short pier?' said Primrose.

'Fabulous idea,' said the nannies, and stumped off towards the harbour.

Clink.

'What's *in* those sweeties?' said Daisy, marching over the drawbridge.

'Vitriol. Sweet Reason. Essence of Pressure,' said Primrose. 'Down these stairs, right?'

'Here goes,' said Daisy. 'Ugh. This tunnel is in a disgusting state.'

'Deeply slimy.' There was a sploshing. 'And this would be the water. Third on the right, if I'm right, right?'

'Right,' said Daisy. 'Right right here.'

She raised her voice. 'Coo-eee! Pete, er, Nanny Petronella?'

'Over here!' cried a voice.

They were walking along a passage of weeping stone, lined on both sides with iron-bound oak doors. Most of the little barred windows were full of groans. The window of cell five was full of Pete's face, crossish under its bowler hat. 'What kept you?' he said.

'All things come to him who waits,' said Daisy primly. She took the key down from the nail and opened the door. 'Are you all right, Pete?'

'Very comfy,' said Pete. 'Barring the odd newt and similar.'

'Any luck with your search for the missing?'

'Not as such,' said Pete, avoiding her eye.

'Dearie me,' said Daisy. 'Shall we go?'

'Er . . .' said Primrose, as if trying to attract her attention.

'This is no time for saying "Er",' said Daisy, sharply. 'Oh.'

For the corridor was suddenly full of vast nannies, towering over Primrose like an overhang of rock.

'Peppermint?' said Primrose, holding out the tin.

'Oo, nice, ta, don't mind if I do,' said the lead nanny, reaching out a huge hand.

A huge and clumsy hand.

A huge and clumsy hand that knocked the peppermints out of Primrose's grasp and on to the passage floor, where a huge and clumsy brogue crushed them into the wet slime.

'Oops, dearie me,' said the lead nanny.

'Oops,' said Daisy.

'What are you doing here?' said the lead nanny.

'We came to see our mate, er, colleague nanny, er, Petronella,' said Primrose.

'So we could torture him a bit,' said Daisy hastily.

'Ever so nice,' said the lead nanny. 'Password?'

'Rockabye baby.'

There was a short, deep silence. 'The password changes at half past ten,' said the lead nanny sweetly. 'It is now quarter to eleven.' The great head bowed towards Daisy and Primrose. 'Naughty, naughty,' said the head.

Daisy looked at her watch. 'I make it twenty-eight minutes past –'

Huge hands grabbed them and thrust them into Pete's cell. The door closed with a slam. 'Nighty-night,' said a gravel voice through the barred window. 'Tomorrow, I am sure that people will want to ask you some questions. Quite a lot of questions.'

'Hard ones,' said another voice.

Locks turned. Bolts shot. Chains clanked. Brogues crunched in the corridor, fading. Then there was absolute, complete darkness, like the inside of a cow but much, much colder.

'Nighty-night to you too,' said Primrose, definitely not meaning it.

There was a silence. Daisy felt rather sad. They were absolutely no closer to finding the Chief and Papa Darling. Further away, actually. In a deep, deep cellar under the ground, with no light and a hole in the floor instead of a lav, and very nasty people outside who were going to ask them hard questions. But she forced herself to look on the sunny side, what there was of it in the pitch-black cell.

'Well!' she said brightly. 'There must be a way out.'

'The door,' said Pete. 'It's locked.'

Daisy felt her way round the walls. They were made of massive stone, tightly jointed. The floor seemed to be slimy concrete. The ceiling was more stone, vaulted. 'Yes,' she said, unable to stop a small niggle of despair. 'I see.' She sat down on the rough stone bench. 'All right, Prim?'

'Cool,' said her sister's voice from the darkness beside her.

Silence fell, a rather gloomy silence, broken only by the sound of dripping water. Finally, Daisy said, 'We might as well sing.'

'Sing what?'

Pause. Then Primrose said, 'What about "Burglars Rejoice"?'

'Nice one,' said Pete. 'A-one, two, three.'

And off they went, their voices bright and clear in the dark:

Burglars Rejoice, the sun has just gone down,
So off we run to see what we can half-inch in this town –
All fingers crossed, and here is definitely hopin'
For punters with eyes shut and ground-floor windows open.
Oooo, up with the ladder,
In*to the house,*
Tip*toe along,*
Quiet *as a mouse.*
Look at them sparklers
Exceedingly choice.
Into the swagbag –
Oh, Burglars Rejoice!

They sang all the verses. Then they sang the 'Safecracker's Explosion' and the 'Pickpocket's

Packet'. The last notes fell dead into the darkness. And once again there was silence and dripping water.

Daisy felt a hand in hers. Then she felt another hand in her other hand. Daisy, Primrose and Pete sat in the dark and listened to the drips. The sunny side was completely invisible. They did not feel all that happy. Hardly happy at all. All right, not even a tiny bit –

Clink.

– happy.

Clink.

'What was that?' said Daisy.

Clink.

'Sort of clink noise,' said Pete.

Clink.

'Like someone bashing a stone with a pickaxe,' said Primrose.

'Chisel, actually,' said someone.

'We haven't got a chisel.'

'I have,' said the new voice.

The cell exploded into light.

'Sorry,' said the voice. 'Hope I no dazzle you. It often happen when I come into a room.'

'And who,' said Daisy, with her eyes shut, 'might you be?'

'Because we are very glad to see you, whoever you are,' said Pete hastily.

Daisy opened her eyes. As they got used to the dazzle, she saw a lit candle on top of a tin helmet. Under the helmet was a boy of about eleven with a brown face, large brown eyes and spiky black hair that stuck out from under the brim. 'Good evening,' said the boy. 'I am El Gusano, which means The Worm, an ironical name because in fack I am action hero.'

'How do you do?' said Daisy politely.

'I am always in excellent shape,' said El Gusano. 'Would you like to get out of here?'

'Indeed we would,' said Daisy.

El Gusano stood up and waved a courteous hand at the wall. The cellmates observed that a stone had been pushed out, and that behind it was darkness, with a pong of sewage. 'Then if you would be so good as to follow me,' he said.

'Yuk,' said Daisy.

'Fusspot,' said Pete.

'Let's *go*,' said Primrose.

They looked at the hole. It looked small, dark and smelly. But then so did the cell.

They took a deep breath. They crammed their

bowler hats down over their ears. Into the hole they went, following the yellow light of their saviour's helmet candle.

'Where are we going?' said Daisy.

'Elsewhere,' said Primrose.

'Keep moving,' said Pete.

The sewers of Ciudad Olvidada smelt slightly better than the streets of Ciudad Olvidada, because it was the kind of city where what was supposed to be in the sewers was mostly left lying about in the streets. Daisy and Primrose would have liked a chat about the luckiness of their escape and the mysteriousness of El Gusano. But the little brown boy led them at astonishing speed through tunnels, up ladders, round corners, and once, for a short period, along the bank of a river down which were carried uprooted palm trees, on one of which was a sweet monkey. Primrose would have absolutely loved to take the monkey home and teach it to cook and perhaps to bite people she did not like. But El Gusano cried, '¡Pronto!' and directed them into another pipe.

After twenty minutes' weary sploshing, the pipe came to an end. El Gusano pushed upward at the ceiling. A trapdoor swung up and a stepladder swung down. At the top of the ladder they found themselves in a bathroom of greenish stone with dripping walls.

'Where are we?' said Daisy.

'In the famous marble lavatory of the Dictatabunker,' said El Gusano. 'Was used by the guy before the guy before the guy before last who ran the country. Was scared one day it would start raining big big stones from outer space. Now is empty, or so they think, but of course I am far too clever for them.'

'Wha?' said Primrose.

'Follow me,' said El Gusano. He led them into a hall of slimy stone. In a pointed archway was a tall door. 'Welcome,' he said, flinging the door open.

Once, it might have been a bunker used for tennis. Now it was a bunker full of bunks. There was a roar of voices, which stilled as the Darlings and Pete came into the room. El Gusano led them to a small side cave where the bunks had a peculiarly luxurious air, being covered in red velvet with gold tassels. 'You want food?' he said. 'We have boiled beans, salt-free, very healthy, made by El Cook.' He pointed to a bulging person wearing a bean-stained apron.

'Yuk,' said Primrose.

El Cook scowled at her.

'Bit late for us,' said Daisy, yawning hastily. 'We must get back to the ship.'

'The Nanas will be lookin' for you. First, you sleep,' said El Gusano. 'Myself, I hardly sleep at all, because I am naturally very strong, and also have a will of iron. In the mornin', to the ship.' He left, hauling the door shut behind him.

Daisy noted that he did not lock it. A good sign.

'Nice gaff,' said Pete. 'If you like slime.'

'Beans!' snorted Primrose.

All that came from Daisy's bed was a deep, elegant snore.

When Daisy opened her eyes, she became aware of quite a lot of things all at once. There was a rather ghastly smell, as of nearby sewers and many children. Pete and Primrose's bunks were empty. And there was a huge noise coming from somewhere out of sight. She pulled on her dress, padded over the damp flagstones and followed the noise.

Outside the door El Cook stood in her way, all bulges and unspeakable apron. 'We eat beans and only beans,' he said. 'But look what she done.' He seemed to be about to cry.

Daisy had no idea what he was talking about. She said, 'Be big and brave,' in her most nannyish voice, and pushed past him.

Primrose was by a stove at the far end of the room, dishing out eggs, sausages, tomatoes, fried bread and something that looked suspiciously like haunch of venison from a gigantic pan. There was cereal to start, with yogurt or double cream or both, and toast and peach jam to finish.

As the children got their breakfasts, the hum of conversation stopped. The only sounds were people saying 'Yum' and 'Sloo' and 'More'.

Daisy moved on to a bench beside Pete. 'I thought they only ate beans,' she said. 'Where did all this food come from?'

'Found it,' said Pete.

'Found it?'

Pete's gaze shifted under Daisy's piercing eye. 'Orright,' he said. 'I got up early and half-inched it.'

'Wha?'

'Half-inched, pinched.'

'From where?'

'Convoy of lorries. Driving up the road towards the mountains.' Pete waved a hand at the ceiling, where a bright bar of sunlight fell through a drain grating. 'I sort of knocked off the last lorry in the line.'

'Hey!' cried a voice. 'Good morning!' It was El Gusano, with admiration in his eye and sausage grease in his ear. 'El Cook sulking.'

'Never mind,' said Daisy. She indicated the many children. 'Tell me, who are all of you?'

'It is a sad story,' said El Gusano. 'We are the Lost Children of Nananagua.'

'Lost?'

'We know where we are, of course. But the government does not. And our parents do not.'

'Your parents?'

El Gusano shook his head. 'My father is called El Presidente Real Banana. There was a revolution. The Nanas, those nasty people in uniforms you have seen, took over the country, to make it safe, they said, but of course they only wanted power. They locked up my father and other government people, who are the parents of the other Lost Children here. They left three government people, who are the Junta, who are very powerful and who have the job to turn the ideas of Las Nanas into laws.'

'So you escaped the Nanas?' said Daisy.

'For a genius like me, was not difficult,' said El Gusano. 'We slided down the drainpipes and went underground, where they are too fat to follow. My father had told me about this bunker, so now there are eighty of us who live here. We watch Las Nanas and we stay out of the way and we creep through the drains, and sometimes we rescue good peoples who fall into the hands of Las Nanas and the Junta.'

'Ah,' said Daisy, who on the whole preferred people to be more modest than El Gusano.

'And we set traps,' said El Gusano. 'Sometimes we get one. But the Nanas are strong and wary, and they are suspicious. And the other kids are kind of, I don't want no trouble.'

'The Flying Nanny!' exclaimed Daisy. 'That was you?'

El Gusano shrugged. 'Brilliant, was it not?' he said.

'Very clever,' said Daisy rather coolly.

'Anyway, we plan to overthrow the Junta,' said El Gusano. 'To get rid of Las Nanas. To get our parents back. To bring back a good government headed by my daddy, El Presidente Real Banana, the Popular Choice.' He shrugged. 'We are only children, though of course I am a genius. I always tell the others, we may be crawling through the sewers but sometimes through a drain grating we see the moon. The others are like, we are doomed, and the food is terrible.'

'Courage!' cried Daisy. 'Let us make a deal!'

'Deal?'

'We will clean you up and help you get your parents back. And you will help us get our Chief Engineer and the key to the ship. The Chief Engineer has been kidnapped –'

'And Papa,' said Primrose.

'Him too. Now, Gusano. How would you seek missing persons in this country of yours?'

'I would ask me. At which point I, El Gusano, would make enquiries, which would probably be very very successful.'

'Excellent!' cried Daisy. 'That is exactly what we will do!'

'By the way,' said Primrose. 'Have you ever heard of someone called the Great One?'

El Gusano's eyes widened, and his mouth opened, and his face paled beneath its coating of drain scum. 'The Great One?' he said. 'Er . . .'

'Is something wrong?'

El Gusano seemed to be about to say something.

But he turned it into a light laugh. 'Wrong? Me? No!' he cried. 'Never heard of no Great One. And you don' want to neither. Now forward! To victory! For El Gusano is on the case!'

The Chief loved his new bedroom. There was a four-poster bed with rich red velvet curtains sweeping up to a wonderfully shiny crown. There was a coal fire and a rocking chair by the fender. There were a lot of very big people in some sort of uniform who bowed low before him and took away his uniform to be washed and gave him a splendid garment that some people would have called a dressing gown but he knew was actually a Robe of State. There was apparently a volcano close at hand and codfish for lunch, though it seemed there was a bit of trouble about lunch, because he had heard them talking about it. Naughty people had stolen a lorry with food in it. But this was far beneath the Chief's attention.

What mattered was this.

The Royal Edward had his own small throne by the fire.

The staff treated him with Correct Deference. (Here the Chief poked the Royal Edward in the stomach. The Royal Edward said, 'GOOT EVENINK, YOUR ROYAL HIGHNESS.' 'Loff you too!' said the Chief.)

And the sweet familiar voice was calling him. *Your Royal Highnesses!* it cried. *Eat your nice codfish all up, like you used to at Kodsfjord, and we will go to see the volcano! Soooooooooon! And when you are ready, give me the keeeeeeey!*

Happy, happy, *happy*!

Except about the key, of course.

4

It was quiet on the quay at ten o'clock that night. Sergeant Fantastico was sitting with his back against a low wall, swigging rum and smoking a cigar. The *Kleptomanic II* was blacked out, except for a couple of floodlights that shone in Sergeant Fantastico's eyes and made it hard for him to see what was happening on deck. Not that Sergeant Fantastico was bothered. He and Bingo and El Garrote were supposed to be making sure that no one escaped heavenly Nananagua on to the

Kleptomanic. But he and Bingo and El Garrote were not the kind of policemen who wanted to police anybody. They were the kind of policemen who wanted quiet weeks that they got paid at the end of. Which meant they were the kind of policemen who kept an eye out for Las Nanas, because you did not want to get on the wrong side of Las Nanas, no way. And the lights on this ship shone over the quay, so you could see Las Nanas coming a mile off, unless they crept up behind one of the cranes, and they did not have the brains to creep up behind cranes.

Hey, thought Sergeant Fantastico, who was none too bright himself. I am a poet, and I do not know it. He began to make up rhymes. Moon, June, he thought. Er, baboon. Whales, bales, emails. He had another swig of rum and felt sorry for himself. Nobody *understood* what it was *like* to be a poet –

'VA-VA-VOOM!' cried a great voice from the *Kleptomanic*'s loudspeakers. 'We PROUDLY PRESENT . . . LA NANA!'

A searchlight beam lanced out from the ship's bridge. It lit up something dangling from a crane.

Sergeant Fantastico felt the night air inside his mouth. What was dangling from the crane had black shoes and a greenish dress and a brown bowler hat.

Clink, went a manhole cover on the quay behind him.

Many emotions collided under Sergeant Fantastico's tunic. It was frankly great to see a Nana slung from a crane. But if any other Nanas saw it, there would be . . . well, he did not like to think what there would be, but in his mind he heard cell doors slamming and the creak of thumbscrews.

He found he was running towards the crane. And the other policemen from the gangway were running with him.

Clink, went a manhole cover on the quay behind him.

'Now!' hissed a voice.

Sergeant Fantastico stood with his comrades under the crane. None of them knew where to look. Obviously up was out of the question, in case they saw the Nana's knickers. But down was out of the question too, in case they were accused of Not Paying Attention. So they looked at each other. Finally Bingo, whose mother had been an ape, started to climb the ladder to the control cab.

Somewhere behind them on the quay, there was a *clank*. The policemen paid no attention.

'All clear,' said El Gusano.

Daisy stuck her head out of the manhole. The quay stretched away in all directions under the stars. There was the crane and the dangling Nana and the policemen milling around looking useless. And there were the homely white upperworks of the *Kleptomanic*. 'Very neat,' she said, and heaved herself out of the hole. 'Quickly now, children.'

From the darkness below came the shuffling of many, many feet.

'Lower away!' cried Sergeant Fantastico.

Bingo yanked the first lever that came to hand. The dangling Nana suddenly became a plummeting Nana. She landed with a thump and lay still.

'Ono!' cried Sergeant Fantastico, not because he was sad but because he could not bear to think what would happen to him when the Nanas found out about this.

El Garrote had no imagination, and therefore no worries. He walked over to the Nana and stirred it with his toe. 'Not alive,' he said.

'We *keeled* it?'

'Never was alive,' said El Garrote. 'So not dead, because only something that has been alive can be –'

'Shadaaaap!' cried Sergeant Fantastico, taking in the painted face, the dented bowler, the stockinged – no, *sacking* – legs, leaking . . . *sand*. An *imitation* Nana.

He turned.

He turned just in time to see the last of a procession of small figures trotting up the gangway of the *Kleptomanic II*. It was wearing a tin helmet with a candle stuck to the top.

They had been tricked. By children.

Sergeant Fantastico reckoned they had two choices. Choice one was to tell the Great One that due to a bit of difficulty lots of Nananaguan kids had escaped on to the ship. Sergeant Fantastico shivered, hearing in his mind the cell-door-and-thumbscrew noises.

Choice two was to stay shtumm.

Choice two got his vote every time.

He said to El Garrote, 'What did we see?'

'Werl,' said El Garrote. 'There was this sand fing wearing Nana gear. Plus kids. Lorra lorra kids –'

'We saw *nothing*,' said Sergeant Fantastico.

'But –'

'*Nothing*,' said Sergeant Fantastico. 'If you thought you saw something you were wrong. We saw *nothing*.'

'Oh.' El Garrote was used to being wrong. 'Nuffink.'

'Correct.'

Bingo came down the ladder. 'Cor,' he said. 'Did you see all them little bleeders getting on to the ship?'

'No,' said Sergeant Fantastico, scowling horribly. 'Hint.'

Bingo was not all that clever, but he was clever enough for this. 'Yeah,' he said. 'Me too. Nuffink.'

'Well then,' said Sergeant Fantastico. 'Back on guard, eh?'

An hour later, El Gusano's attractive but eccentric candle helmet had been removed, he had been vigorously scrubbed and fed another of Primrose's most delicious meals. He was on the *Kleptomanic*'s bridge, bowing deeply to the Captain. He said, 'Beautiful lady, I thank you for the hearty welcome you have extended to me and my *compadres*.'

The Captain smiled vaguely. Sophie Nickit and

the girl burglars, who were watching through the window, nudged each other. They thought he was sweet.

'So,' said the Captain. 'We are delighted to offer you food and shelter while we do what we have to do. Apparently you have been making enquiries about our Chief.'

'Yes,' said El Gusano. 'An' obviously I have been very very successful.'

'You have?' said the Darlings as one Darling.

'Yep. My sources say a big fat guy with a spike hat went ashore. He got in a big big car. And was driven away.'

'And?' said Primrose.

'Who by?'

'Where to?'

'Grammar,' sighed the Captain.

'All this is not important,' said El Gusano. 'But I will tell you because I am generous. This was a big big big car. Apparently it belonged to one of the Junta.'

'A junta,' said the Captain, 'is a little group of important people who run rather backward countries.'

'Like I already tol' you,' said El Gusano.

'But what,' said the Captain, 'would they want with the Chief?'

'Amazingly, I dunno,' said El Gusano.

'But we will find out,' said Daisy. 'Tell me, Gusano, do these . . . Junta people have children?'

'Of course.'

'Do they look after these children themselves?'

'Don' be silly. They are far too important. They have nannies.'

'Nanas?'

'Very similar. But nannies too small and weak to be in Las Nanas so have not been selected by the G–' He stopped.

'By whom?' said Daisy, fixing him with a steely eye.

'Spit it out,' said Primrose.

'You were going to say Great One,' said Daisy. 'Weren't you?'

El Gusano's face was ashen, his voice low. 'I am the bravest person I have ever met,' he said. 'But even I know that there are some things in this country that are too frightening to talk about.'

The lady burglars battered open the window and leaned in. 'Aah,' they said. 'Leave it out, Daisy, poor boy, innit.'

Daisy bowed. Perhaps she had gone too far. 'Well,' she said, 'we can leave the Great One for the moment. Meanwhile, to find the Chief it seems we must first get close to the Junta.'

'How?' said the Captain.

Daisy said, 'I feel that dreadful things will soon start happening to the nannies of the Junta. And we will be on hand to Step In.'

'Well!' said the Captain brightly. 'That's settled, then!'

Bingo's two-way radio was crackling.

'Yeah?' he said.

'Word from above,' said the voice of his sergeant. 'Someone's nicked one of the Great One's lorries. With the Great One's special supplies on. The Great One is not pleased.'

'The Great One?' said Bingo. 'Blimey. Who'd nick one of the Great One's lorries?'

'Probably another revolution,' said the voice. 'Ten-four, then.'

'Ten-four,' said Bingo gloomily.

Cassian and El Gusano spent the evening in the ship's welding shop. And Daisy, Primrose and Pete ironed their nanny outfits and prepared for action.

Tomorrow was going to be a busy day.

There were three people in the Junta. There was El Generalissimo, who was in charge of the Army. There was Minister Dollar, who was in charge of Finance, meaning the Money. And there was El Simpatico, who was in charge of Health and Safety.

For the nannies who looked after the children of the Junta the following day started like any other.

It did not go on that way.

5

Nanny Potter was a genuine rawhide-tough graduate of the Nanny Academy. She looked after the children of El Generalissimo. That day, she rose early and swung into her invariable routine. Breakfast of grapefruit, biltong and bitter chocolate. Then salute the picture of the pink-faced nanny on the wall and off to rouse her little charges.

Stalin and Napoleon (their daddy had chosen the names) were seven years old and small for their age. They were pale little boys, with a pinched and furtive air, as if afraid someone would shout at them. Asleep, they twitched faintly. Stalin even smiled, perhaps remembering his mother, who had run away shortly after El Generalissimo had taken to wearing full military uniform in bed.

At eight o'clock, Nanny Potter stood with her hands on her hips, scowling down at the sleeping tinies. Small thoughts moved sluggishly in her thick skull. *The early bird catches the worm. Naughty, naughty. Early to bed and early to rise makes a man healthy and wealthy and wise.*

The little boys seemed to feel the weight of her thoughts. Their eyes flicked open. They leaped out of bed and stood to attention and piped in their thin little voices, 'GOOD MORNING, NANA, FUNNY OLD WEATHER WE ARE HAVING FOR THE TIME OF YEAR.'

'At ease,' growled the nanny. 'Stand easy.' She rolled up her sleeves.

'Nooo!' cried Stalin.

But remorseless nanny hands grabbed him, lifted him and dunked him into a huge enamel bath full of icy water.

'Aaargh!' cried Stalin.

'Eeek!' cried Napoleon, being dunked too.

But remorseless nanny hands grasped a huge wooden scrubbing brush and a bar of yellow soap and scrubbed the tiny brothers without mercy.

Then there was Putting On Uniforms and Tying Shoelaces, leaving ends exactly 33 millimetres long. Then there was Breakfast, which was last week's bread soaked in watered-down milk. After Breakfast, boots crashed outside the door.

'Must we?' whimpered the little ones.

'Of course you must!' cried the nanny. 'Now, be off with you and do your nice Military Training!' She flung the door open.

The sergeant major stamped in with an atomic crash of boots. 'Squaad!' he roared. 'Squaaad – 'SHUN!'

The little boys shuffled their feet together.

'HOW TALL ARE YOU?' roared the sergeant major.

'One metre,' squeaked Napoleon.

'NEVER SEEN RUBBISH PILED SO HIGH IN ME LIFE,' bellowed the sergeant major.

Stalin gave a small, nervous squeak.

'OI!' roared the sergeant major. 'YOU! SHURRUP OR I WILL STICK MY STICK

UP YOUR NOSE AND *TWIDDLE*! Now. By the LEFT. Quick MARCH!' Twirling his moustache and winking at Nanny Potter, he marched his little charges out of the room.

Nanny Potter spent a short time blushing and simpering. A fine figure of a man, that sergeant major, she thought. Oo yes. She finished her cuppa and went out for her morning walk.

Nanny Potter was a creature of iron and whipcord. She was also a creature of habit. The route of her walk did not vary, and nor did its purpose. She went straight past the soldiers guarding the front gate, straight down the hill and straight along Presidential Avenue to the El Superbo Apartments, home of her friend Nanny Cringe. Every day, Nanny Potter and Nanny Cringe drank tea and talked about What the World Was Coming To, the Need for Discipline, a Healthy Diet and Ever Fiercer Nannying. They had started with children, but hoped in time to be promoted to the ranks of Las Nanas. And even (they whispered sometimes) to have tea with the Great One.

Today was a tiny bit different, of course. The lower orders had been at it again. Apparently her friend and star pupil Nanny Dangerfield had had a bit of trouble involving a crane, a 5-kilometre accidental flight and a fist-fight with some sharks. Lovely woman, Nanny Dangerfield. Nanny Potter was very proud of her. Potter had remained a humble nanny, but Dangerfield had risen like a rocket into the upper ranks of the Nanas and was now very, very close to the Great One. Nanny Dangerfield had been talking mysteriously about Great Events, a Special Guest and Changes In Store. Nanny Potter had had her own experience of Special Guests these last few days. She could hardly wait for a good gossip about these matters.

As she had these thoughts, she was passing under a crane. She noticed that the crane hook was down at road level. Attached to the hook was a platform. Sitting on the platform was a figure in a crude cardboard bowler hat, a nanny dress and a pair of clumsily painted black brogues. There was a sign round its neck. AL NANYS AR BUM, said the sign. Tch, thought Nanny Potter, marching onward. Too clever by half, all this writing. Must think I was born yesterday. She would call the officers from Nanny Cringe's, and heads would roll, oh yes.

Clink, went something behind her.

Nanny Potter whirled on her brogue heels.

There was only the avenue stretching away under the hot sun, a dotted line of manhole covers leading back to the Old Town, the Caboose crouching on its hill like a flaky white toad.

Nanny Potter marched into the lobby of the El Superbo Apartments.

It was a nice lobby. Unlike the rest of Nananagua it was clean and smelt slightly of disinfectant. It had a marble floor and the usual picture of the pink-faced nanny on the wall. A notice said REPORT TO THE RECEPTIONIST. There was no one at the reception desk, of course. Nanny Potter detected Slipping Standards. She thought about having a good look round, in case there was someone skulking. But it was at least half an hour since Nanny Potter had had any tea, and she was thirsty. So she headed for the lift.

Reader, Nanny Potter's thirst had betrayed her. Had she not been in such a hurry, she would have looked behind the desk. Had she looked behind the desk, she would have seen the receptionist, bound and gagged, trying to shout with his eyes. She would also have seen a mess of tools and wires and some very oily handprints, and spared herself a truly remarkable experience.

She did none of the above. On she ploughed, to her date with Destiny.

A warning sign said THIS LIFT MAY GO UP AS WELL AS DOWN. She pressed the lift button. The doors opened. She pressed the button marked PENTHOUSE. She felt the pressure on her brogue soles as the lift started upward. Nanny Potter licked her lips. She could almost taste the tea. Four, five, said the floor indicator. She waited for the lift to slow down.

The lift did not slow down.

Actually, it seemed to get faster. Six and seven flashed past in a blur. The upward G-force on her brogue soles was trying to telescope her legs. Nanny Potter's jaw dropped, partly from astonishment and partly from acceleration. The floor indicator smoked, glowed and exploded. There was a second, much bigger crash. The upward movement continued. Through a hole that had appeared in the side of the lift, Nanny Potter saw clouds and seagulls. The lift rocketed into the sky, tilting as it soared. Far below, Nanny Potter saw the roof of the El Superbo Apartments. There was a hole where the top of the lift shaft should have been. Next to the hole were two small figures. One was brown and wearing a tin helmet, and was of course El Gusano. The other was black with what looked like engine oil, and was of course Cassian. They were both looking up. There was a toolbox between them. They were shaking hands.

The lift with Nanny Potter in it soared up and up, trailing cables. When it was over the sea, Nanny Potter found she was weightless. Then gravity took hold. The lift stopped soaring. It began to plummet.

Far below, a party of sharks moved into position.

It looked like lunchtime.

Back at the official residence of El Generalissimo, the tinies were returning from drill. There was a new nanny, thickset and badly shaved. ''Ello, saucepans!' said the nanny. 'I am Nanny Pete, and you are in luck! First, elevenses. Then you can tell me what you've been doing!'

They had delicious cocoa and buns. Then little Napoleon and Stalin brought Pete up to date with the doings of the household. Yes, they said, they had had a very important visitor two nights ago. They had been allowed to look at him a bit. They took Pete to a spare room.

'Look!' said Stalin.

'Teef!' said Napoleon.

And sure enough, there on the golden bedstead were the marks of a set of large, crunching, peg-like teeth.

Pete had seen those toothmarks on the *Kleptomanic*, in places where the Chief had got overexcited. He recognized them immediately.

They were the Cheeth's tief.

The Chieth's teef.

Whatever.

The Chief was all warm and dark, and someone was telling him a story.

Once upon a tiiiiiiiiime, said the voice, *there was a nanny, and what a lovely job she'd got, with children on a lovely yacht, sailing seas of deepest blue with very little work to do. But wicked parents one sad day drove their yacht into a bay and dumped that nanny and sailed away. Naturally within the hour this clever nanny had seized power and with the power of her right hand reorganized the smelly land. But ever since that tragic time she's felt her stranding was a crime. And crimes must always be put straight; this is the awful will of Fate. So, out of many nooks and crannies, she summoned up the World's Worst Nannies. And using otherworldly powers developed in her idle hours, she summoned from a distant isle the one who'd always made her smile. And now her little Prince was here, grown up into an Engineer! Such fun there'd be! Such merry laughter! They'd both live Happy Ever After. And here's the really lovely thing! She'd turn the Prince into a King! Now if Your Royal Highness please, he should give Nana his yacht's keeeeeeeeeys —*

'NOOOOOOOOOOOOOOOOOOOOOOO!' cried the Chief, grasping the key on the chain round his neck and rolling over so nobody could get at it, ever.

In tiiiiiiime, Your Naughty Royal Highness. In tiiiime.

6

Cecil, Denis and Ariadne Dollar, children of the Minister of Finance, had finished off their hard-boiled eggs and burned toast. Then they had been locked in the nursery of the Casa del Dinero, the Minister's official residence, to Play Quietly while nanny did the ironing.

Playing Quietly was not actually much fun. The nursery was large and bare. It contained a rocking horse, a doll's house and a TV. On the wall was a picture of the usual nanny. In this one she wore a brown bowler hat on top of her silly pink face and the china-blue eyes that followed you round the room. Beside the nanny picture a notice said READING IS DANGEROUS — IT HELPS YOU THINK FOR YOURSELF. Obviously, there were no books. Cecil, Denis and Ariadne were too big for the rocking horse, too bored for the doll's house, and there was nothing on TV in Nananagua except films that told you how everything interesting, such as ice cream or riding or surfing or welding, was either bad for you or not safe.

And even if you did manage to get interested in any of these boring and stupid things, the picture on the wall gave you a clammy feeling that you were being Bad. The picture on the wall gave you the idea that you should be Sitting Down but Up Straight, saying Prune and Prism silently, and being Good. It was a really dreadful picture. Naturally, the Dollar children had begun to bicker. The bickering had turned into fighting. They were in a mean, gouging ball on the floor when the nursery door opened.

Denis swiftly pulled his spectacles out of his sister's right nostril. Ariadne pulled her hair comb out of Cecil's leg and Cecil removed his ruler from

Denis's ear, and they sprang to attention and tried to look as if red and furious was the natural expression of their faces in repose.

A voice from the doorway said, 'That's them.' It was the voice of El Gusano, known to the Dollar children as Joey Banana.

The Dollar children's mouths fell open. Once, Joey Banana had occasionally come to play, which was cool, because he was a fun guy and a good welder. Then Joey Banana had Disappeared. Disappearing had a special meaning in Nananagua. Nobody would tell you what that special meaning was. All any Nananaguan child knew was that it was special in a way you did not want to find out about.

'I am much obliged to you,' said the other person in the doorway.

The other person in the doorway was a nanny, small and determined-looking, with bright green eyes, perfect nail varnish and a saddle of freckles across her nose. Ariadne was instantly impressed. Denis and Cecil found themselves feeling strangely protective, as if they wished to shelter this nanny from the Storms of Life. This was weird, given what nannies normally did to you.

'Well!' cried the small nanny in a brisk, cheery voice. 'Hello, hello. Where's your nanny?'

'Nanny Devine? Ironing,' said Denis.

'In the ironing room. Down there,' said Cecil, pointing.

'Excellent,' said the nanny, who of course was Daisy. 'Now tell me, dears, have you got a skipping rope?'

'Yep,' said Ariadne gloomily. 'I hate skipping. It's feeble.'

'True,' said Daisy. 'But a skipping rope can be so useful. Give it to me.'

Five minutes later, the door of the ironing room had been firmly but stealthily lashed to the handle of the door opposite.

'Great knot skills!' cried Denis, impressed.

'I have lived on ships,' said Daisy modestly. 'Now then. We have work to do. Which way to the part of the house where they keep the jewels and spoons?'

'This way!' cried the little Dollars, jumping up and down and clapping their hands, they knew not why. And off they went, into the splendid state rooms of the Casa del Dinero.

'By the way,' said Daisy as they walked the endless corridors. 'Have you had any visitors lately?'

'Yes!' cried Denis.

'An enormous one!' cried Cecil. 'He came to tea!'

'Come and look!' cried Ariadne.

The children pulled Daisy, to whom they were already most attached, down a corridor and into a stately drawing room decorated in blue and gold. 'Look at the coffee table!' they cried.

And there in the table were the marks of a set of large, crunching, peg-like teeth.

Daisy had seen those toothmarks on the *Kleptomanic*, in places where the Chief had got overexcited. She recognized them immediately.

They were the Chieth's teef.

The Cheeth's tief.

Whatever.

Nanny Divine divided the world into people who divided the world into two kinds of people and people who were very, very silly. Nanny Divine divided the world into big nannies and slim nannies. She considered herself a slim nanny. She also divided the world into neat nannies and cosy nannies. She considered herself a neat nanny. Her brogues shone, her apron crackled with starch, and her bowler hat sat dead level over her well-brushed eyebrows. She divided children into good children and bad children. The children of Minister Henry Dollar, Nananagua's Mr Business, had before her arrival been Bad, devoted to horse riding and welding. Nanny Divine had put a stop to all that. Now they were Good. Or anyway she could not hear them from her ironing room, here in the nursery wing of the Casa del Dinero, official residence of the Minister and Madame Dollar. Though admittedly her ironing room was lined eight deep with ironed bath towels and a good long way from the nursery, so Nanny Divine could be peaceful even when the children were nailing each other to the wall by their ears, curse their dark hearts . . .

Wait a minute. First things first.

Nanny Divine switched off her iron and placed it exactly in the middle of the stone plinth provided. She adjusted her eyebrow grooming in the mirror. She had been ironing for hours. It was time for their morning watered-down milk, nasty little gourmandizers. She walked to the ironing-room door, turned the handle and pulled.

Nothing happened.

She pulled again.

Still nothing.

She yanked. She rattled. She kicked, biffed and gave it the knee. Then she charged it with her shoulder.

She wrenched her arm. She hurt her knee. She hurt her shoulder.

She began to roar.

It was a large, full-throated roar. Normally it could bend window glass at a hundred paces. But in the ironing room it was muffled by many layers of wool and towelling. From the nursery you could hardly hear it, from the main house not at all.

A merry hour later, Daisy and the children were back in the nursery, pillowcases bulging. 'Excellent!' said Daisy. 'Cocoa time.'

'We don't have cocoa,' said Denis, who seemed to be some kind of spokesman.

'You do now,' said Daisy. She whipped up cocoa with marshmallows in it, and distributed Primrose's home-made Jaffa Cakes from a tin she had brought. The children grew steadily pinker and happier, despite the roaring and thudding now issuing from the ironing room. 'Well,' said Daisy. 'Let's do it.'

'Do what?' said the children.

But Daisy was already on the internal phone.

'Minister Dollar?' she was saying. 'There is something rather ghastly you should see. Me? I am a well-wisher and a nanny. Your children's nanny, as it happens. The temp one. The children's names? Yes, Denis, Cecil and, no, not Beryl, Minister, Ariadne. Very good. See you in a minute, then.'

Feet thundered on the stairs. A block of security men in dark-blue uniforms and peaked caps marched into the nursery wing. The block split. A man in a grey flannel suit and a woman in a little black two-piece and pearls were revealed. The man was talking into a mobile phone. The woman was dictating to a secretary, who bit his nails in between scribbles. Neither of them looked at the children.

Daisy sized up the situation at a glance. 'All hail, Minister and Madame,' she said. 'Of course one hates to trouble you during your busy day, but there is something I think you ought to see.'

'Yeah?' said the Minister, ending one call and dialling another.

Madame seemed to be planning a lunch menu. 'Lobster, partridges, gooseberry fool and oh my golly gosh,' she said. Scribble, scribble, went the secretary.

For Daisy had shooed one and all into Nanny Divine's appallingly tidy floral bedroom and opened a drawer. 'Look!' she cried, lifting up a set of vast prickly knickers.

'Yuk!' cried Madame Dollar.

'Not the knickers,' said Daisy. 'Underneath.'

From under the knickers came the flicker and glitter of precious stones.

'My diamonds!' cried Madame Dollar.

'Calm down,' said Minister Dollar. He switched off the telephone. 'Probably a mistake, my little silly one. Nanny Divine's references were perfect. She is strict, fair, has worked for three dukes and a minister of health, and comes with the personal recommendation of the Great One –'

'And here,' said Daisy, wrenching a stuffed dog to bits, though she was very intrigued by this mention of the Great One. Sawdust filled the air. Something rattled on the floor.

'My Order of the Jewelled Calculator!' cried the Minister. 'Where is that thieving animal of a woman?'

'I have trapped her in the ironing room,' said Daisy, with quiet pride.

'Nice work!' cried the Minister, seizing the calculator and pinning it to the bosom of his shirt. 'Colonel!'

'Aye!' cried one of the uniforms.

'Get Nanny Divine' – his phone rang – 'and, oh, you know, the Caboose, thumbscrews, the usual, hello?' he said, answering it.

'Aye!' cried the colonel. There was a confused rumbling and bumping and some truly frightful cursing, and Nanny Divine was hustled out of the ironing room and in the general direction of the Caboose.

'Where was I?' said Madame Dollar.

'"Oh your golly gosh",' said the secretary.

Madame Dollar started screaming. The secretary concentrated on nail biting. Finally, Madame Dollar came back to herself. 'Who are these little people?' she said.

'Your children,' said the secretary through a mouthful of thumbnail.

Madame Dollar's eyes swept over her children like a stick rattling along a set of railings. 'But who,' she said in a thin, cold voice, 'will do the children's chores?'

'If I may make a proposal, Madame,' said Daisy, stepping forward with a slight curtsy. 'I have a little experience –'

'But who *are* you?' said Madame Dollar. She was walking again.

Daisy found, rather to her surprise, that she was trotting after Madame Dollar and feeling (how shocking!) a little *flustered*! She summoned up a mental picture of the Captain, cool and elegant. Immediately she felt better.

'I have served a lengthy apprenticeship,' she said. 'I am familiar with childcare and cookery.'

'Yes, yes, obviously I recognize a nanny uniform when I see one,' said Madame Dollar peevishly. 'But what about *references*?'

Daisy drew herself up to her full height. She did not have any references. She was going to have to bluff. She could always say the Great One had sent her. But what if they checked? And who was this Great One anyway? Obviously she could not ask . . . No. She would just have to say that never in all her born days had she been so insulted, and trust to her Strength of Will. But looking at Madame Dollar, touchy as a landmine in basic black, she was by no means sure it would work. She had a vision of the Caboose, full of slime and thumbscrews. This was almost certainly not going to work.

But it was all she could do.

She took a deep breath. She opened her mouth. The efficient black eyes of Madame Dollar were like twin carbon drill bits. With a sinking heart, Daisy started. 'Never in my –'

The doorbell rang.

Madame Dollar made a noise like a wet thumb on a hot stove. A man in a tailcoat who was probably the butler opened the front door, and let in another man, dressed in a grey silk suit and carrying a briefcase.

Daisy became aware that her mouth was hanging open. She shut it with a snap.

The man was Papa Darling.

But this was not the Papa Darling who normally shuffled around the lower-deck lavs of the *Kleptomanic* wearing rubber gloves and a pained expression. This was the sleek Papa Darling who as CEO of Darling Gigantic had won awards for concreting over the last remaining habitat of the Unstriped Tiger.

Daisy said, 'Never in all my born days has anyone asked me for a reference but since you ask, this important person here will, I know, be pleased to supply one.'

Papa Darling was looking straight through her, as he looked straight through everyone in servant's uniform. His eyes now focused. The powerful look left his face. His skin turned dirty white and his mouth fell open. 'Agaga,' he said.

'I *beg* your pardon?' said Madame Dollar, not one to suffer stranglers gladly.

'He is saying that we have known each other for years,' said Daisy.

'Ggg,' said Papa Darling, recovering slightly. 'That is to say, we have been in a same-house habitation situation for a considerable period –'

'He is trying to say,' said Daisy, 'that I used to live with his children.'

'Agaga,' said Papa Darling, slipping back into the strangle zone.

'And that I used to be practically one of the family.'

'In a manner of speaking,' said Papa Darling with a frightful effort. Beads of sweat were running down his forehead. Daisy suspected that while she was certainly doing a little bluffing, Papa had told a very large number of very big lies to get that suit and briefcase in such a short time.

There was a noise on the enormous stairs. The Minister descended, closing his mobile phone with a snap, suddenly all smiles. 'Darling!' he cried. 'I mean, ha ha how amusing, Madame Minister, may

I present to you Mr Colin Darling, our new junior minister?'

An *enormous* number of *gigantic* lies, thought Daisy.

'Oo,' said Madame Dollar, her steely exterior becoming slightly squashy. 'Of what?'

'My exact title has yet to be decided. Perhaps –'

'Sanitation and Public Hygiene,' said Minister Dollar, beaming.

'Oh,' said Madame Dollar, cooling. Her eye fell on Daisy. 'Well, Nanny? What are you waiting for? You know where the nursery is. Go and do some work.' And she swept Papa and the Minister out of the hall and into a room full of suits.

Daisy trotted busily up to look after her little charges. Her head was spinning slightly as she removed the unpleasant nanny portrait from the nursery wall and shut it in a cupboard. But one thing was clear.

She was in the household of a minister, with whom the Chief had come to tea. The appearance of Papa, apparently rather powerful nowadays, was a great bonus. The hunt was on. The scent was powerful.

Forward! thought Daisy.

*

The Royal Edward was helping the Chief with his jigsaw puzzle. At least, the Great One said it was a jigsaw puzzle, but to the Chief it looked like a machine. It was a peculiar sort of jigsaw puzzle. But the picture on the packet was clear. That was because the Great One had drawn it herself. The pump was there. And the aiming device. And the pivot. And the loudspeakers . . . Inside the packet were about a dozen big lumps of various kinds of metal. Most people would have found the puzzle difficult, if not impossible. But the Chief was by no means most people. What the Chief was doing was cutting and banging the lumps of metal into exactly the right shape, and assembling them into something very like the picture on the packet. Except bigger. And more powerful. Because the Great One had said:

1. When the jigsaw is finished, we will visit the wolcano.

2. Nana knows everything, because she brought up Beobulfy Wulfy in the Old Palace at Kodsfjord, and she had always been right then, and nothing had changed. And after we have visited the wolcano you will be king.

3. Hooray!

'Vill soon be finished,' said the Chief to the Edward. The Edward said nothing, as was his custom when left unpoked. 'Und ve go to wolkano.'

Still nothing from the Edward.

'Soon. Ve hope.'

Still nothing. The Chief frowned. He was happy, of course. Puzzles were fun, and bashing metal was always soothing. But he was really longing to see the volcano and have a good bath in some very hot springs.

Sooooooon, said the kind voice far away in his head. *When you finish your lovely puzzle, Your Royal Highness. Sooooooooon.*

Bliss.

7

Little Kazza Simpatico was practising the recorder again. Up the scale she went. Down the scale she went. Up the scale she went. Down the scale she went. Up. Down. Bish, squeak. Up –

By now you will be thinking, any more of this and I will scream. Even reading about recorder practice can do this to a person.

Nanny Clam was not like that. Nanny Clam sat in her comfy chair in the nursery at the Villa Politico, brogues to the fire, knitting something toothpaste-pink and very prickly. Soon it would be time to give Kazza her lunch. Today it was whole wholemeal sandwiches with cress fragments and absolutely no butter. There would be a pint of foaming cod liver oil to wash it down, and a brilliant green apple for pudding. Then it would be an afternoon in front of Health TV for Kazza while Nanny Clam caught up with some important horse racing. Splendid, thought Nanny Clam, posting a custard cream between her brownish teeth. Nice to see a little girl brought up as a little girl should be brought up. She tilted back her gargoyle head and smiled at the pictures above the fireplace.

There was the usual pink nanny. Beside the nanny, El Simpatico, the Minister for Health and Safety, smiled right back at Nanny Clam. It was a sweet and thrilling smile in the middle of a kindly face with eyes that twinkled with friendly concern for one and all. Such a *lovely* man, thought Nanny Clam. Him and his tidy friend Derek. Busy, of course, but he was one of the three most important people in Nananagua (after the Great One), so what did you expect? It was so nice that everyone was kept safe and so beautifully in order . . .

Nanny Clam returned to herself. Her heavy brows sank over her piggy eyes. The squeak and bish of the recorder had ceased. Practice time was until one o'clock. It was only twenty to.

Most people would have breathed words of thanksgiving. Not Nanny Clam. She rose and marched out of her cosy sitting room and into the corridor. DANGER OF ELECTRIC SHOCK, said the light bulbs. CAUTION − DOOR, said the doors. BEWARE − HARD WHEN FALLEN ON, said the floor. Turning the thickly padded doorknob, Nanny Clam marched into the nursery.

And stopped.

Kazza was there all right, on her high stool with the training rails, with her spectacles, hairclips, train-track teeth braces, fingernails cut short so she would not scratch herself, clean everything so she would catch no horrid disease. The little girl's eyes shifted guiltily away from Nanny Clam's. On the wall was another picture of the nanny with the pink face and the eyes that followed you round the room, waiting for you to Do Wrong.

The other pair of eyes in the room did not.

They were mild and blue, and they rested coolly upon Nanny Clam from under the brim of a brown bowler hat. 'What ho, Nanny,' said the little pink mouth, with a mild smile.

'And who,' said Nanny Clam through lips like a bird's bottom, 'are you?'

'They call me Nanny Prim,' said Primrose, for it was she. 'Thought I'd drop by and rattle your cage.'

'Rattle . . . my . . . wha?' said Nanny Clam, to whom no one had spoken like this, ever.

'Careful,' hissed Kazza to Primrose in a tiny, tiny voice.

Primrose's small pink hand gripped hers strengtheningly. 'Yeah?' she said. 'And what exactly is it about this weird old trambo that I should be careful *of* ?'

Kazza would rather have jumped into boiling water (DANGER – HOT!) than answer that. Primrose gave a large, pleasant nanny smile. 'Well, anyway,' she said, 'I just thought I'd drop in. We met in the Old Country.'

'Oh?'

'At Her Majesty's. Don't you remember?'

'Ooooh,' said Nanny Clam, making a noise like a punctured owl. Like all nannies, from the greatest to the least, royalty made her all weak at the knees. She had never actually been to Her Majesty's in the

Old Country. But it was very nice that this . . . well, this *attractive* little nanny . . . thought she had. Suddenly Nanny Clam felt proud and strong.

'Bicky?' said Primrose, holding out a tin. 'Right-hand side.'

'How kind,' said Nanny Clam, with her best royal manners. She grasped a dainty handful and stuffed them in her mouth. 'Hev you been in Nananagua long?'

''Bout a week,' said Primrose. 'Feels like years.'

This was a flippant answer. Nanny Clam chewed grimly. She disapproved of flippancy, even from nannies who had worked for royalty. So she was surprised suddenly to find herself laughing so heartily that the picture of the pink nanny vibrated tinnily on the nursery wall.

Kazza shivered. She found nanny laughter very unfamiliar and horribly scaring. Also, the pink nanny in the picture did not seem to approve. She said, 'I want, er, please may I have my . . . nice . . . lunch?'

Primrose had noticed a table bearing a knife, fork, glass, jug of water and something under a check napkin. She peered under the napkin. 'Wholemeal bread, no butter, two pathetic leaves of cress.

Cardboard, cod liver *what*?' she said. 'Stodge. Slime. You can't eat that.' She offered her biscuit tin, which was giving off a delicious smell. 'Left-hand side,' she said. 'Pasties. Go on.'

'But I'm not allowed,' said Kazza.

'Dear oh dear,' said Primrose, fingering her chin in a meditative manner. 'Course you are. Isn't she, Nanny?'

'Course!' cried Nanny Clam, who since her handful of bickies suddenly felt much better. Her eyes were glazed, her grin fixed, and she spoke in a bracing bellow.

'Now, Nanny,' said Primrose, while Kazza munched. 'I think you ought to pop downstairs and tell the bosses exactly what you think.'

'About what?'

'Not being allowed a free hand. Being told what's what.'

A strange light began to burn in Nanny Clam's tiny eye. 'By gum,' she said, slapping her knee. 'You're right, you know. Watch me!' And she strode out of the room.

On her hands.

Kazza swallowed the last of her pasty and brushed crumbs from her mouth with a hanky embroidered with sweet elves. 'Gosh,' she said, watching the nanny's huge bottom sway down the corridor in its lime-green rhino-wool knickers. 'What happened?'

'She ate some of my Who Dares Wins Thins,' said Primrose. 'Another pasty?'

Kazza took a pasty and ate it in one. 'You put something in them,' she said, with her mouth full.

'This and that,' said Primrose.

'Aieee!' cried a voice far away in the house, followed by a long, rippling crash.

'Oo,' said Kazza. 'She must be swinging on the chandelier! *Naughty!*' She frowned. 'I ought to be shocked, but I'm not. What did you put in that pasty?'

'Steak,' said Primrose. 'Onions. One feels better after a good lunch.'

'BANZAI!!' cried a great voice in the distance. There was a rending noise, followed by a gigantic splash and a horrified shriek.

'Down the curtains and into the ornamental pool, by the sound of it,' said Kazza, her poor little eyes now much brighter. 'That was Derek shrieking. Shall we go and have a look?'

Hand in hand, nanny and patient skibbled

through the green baize door and on to the landing.

'See?' said Kazza.

The front hall of the Villa Politico had been arranged to look calm and serene. It had a dome, a marble floor, velvet curtains, an ornamental fountain and a massive staircase. But it was no longer as calm and serene as it was supposed to be. As Kazza had rightly guessed, the chandelier lay smashed on the paving, the curtains were ripped down the middle and the nanny was in the ornamental fountain. A slim man in very tight trousers was crouched on the floor with his face in his hands.

'That's Derek,' said Kazza.

Standing looking at the nanny was a man in a dark suit. He looked exactly like the man in the portrait of El Simpatico, except that his eyes were more like gun barrels than twinkly little stars. He was saying something to Nanny Clam in a low, cold hiss like a snake's. Nanny Clam was laughing heartily at him. She scooped up water in her bowler hat and threw it at him playfully.

'Guards!' roared El Simpatico, foaming with rage.

The hall filled with the tramp of boots. Men in

uniform came and took Nanny Clam away. She put up quite a fight.

'Mission accomplished,' said Primrose, leaning over the upstairs banisters. 'By the way, have you had any visitors here lately?'

'Yes!' cried Kazza, sounding thrilled. 'A really weird one!'

'Sounds about right,' said Primrose, trotting after Kazza, who was leading her down the passage to a room containing a large, throne-like chair.

'They all asked him questions,' said Kazza. 'He made sort of hooting noises. Then he got very happy and he bit the chair. Look!'

Primrose looked. Sure enough, there were toothmarks in the gilded wood of the chair's arm. Above the toothmarks someone had screwed on a brass plate. THESE ARE THE TOOTHMARKS OF CROWN PRINCE BEOWULF OF ICELAND, said the plate.

'And then?'

'They took him away. They said he was going to live with the G–'

'Yes?'

'The Gr–'

'Yes? Whisper, if it helps.'

'The Great One,' said Kazza, looking as if she might faint.

'Good,' said Primrose, thinking, Excellent. 'A little more lunch?'

'Oo,' said Kazza, happy again.

They walked back to the nursery and sat down at the table. Half an hour later, Kazza leaned back in her chair and burped. She said, 'My dream is to do Circus Skills. Do you think it would be, er, all right . . . ?'

'Obviously you should be practising daily,' said Primrose, eyeing the shine in her charge's eye, the new roses in her cheeks. Footsteps sounded. 'Here they come.'

The door opened. El Simpatico and Derek appeared.

'Who are you?' said El Simpatico, looking at Primrose down his perfect nose.

'The new nanny,' said Primrose, curtsying.

'Where did you come from?' said El Simpatico. He still looked very cross.

'They sent me,' said Primrose cunningly.

'Who sent you?'

'Oh *honestly*,' said Derek, who was dressed in a silver puffball jacket and skin-tight blue velvet jeans.

'Yak, yak, yak, when we've got new hall *curtains* to choose!'

'Oo,' said El Simpatico. 'Sorry. Well, carry on, er, Nanny. Do what it says on the notices.' A smile appeared on El Simpatico's face. It was huge and radiant, but his eyes sat above it like little black slugs. 'I know you'll like it here.'

Suddenly the smile was gone. 'But where is the Nana?'

'The Nana?'

El Simpatico pointed a shaking finger at the pale square on the nursery wall where the portrait of the pink nanny had once hung.

'Nasty thing!' said Primrose. She was going to add that she had taken it down because it was hideous and frightening. Then she got a feeling that this would not be sensible.

'Her? Nasty?' said El Simpatico in a strangled voice.

Oops, thought Primrose. 'Dirty,' she said hastily. 'Not properly cleaned.'

'Ah!' cried El Simpatico. 'Cleanliness! Vital! Safe!' He beamed, looking relieved. 'Carry on, Nanny!' And he allowed Derek to fuss him out of the room.

'So who *is* that picture of?' said Primrose.

'Some nanny,' said Kazza. 'Gosh, those two are a pain.'

Primrose gazed into her sad brown eyes. 'Are they your parents?' she said, somewhat mystified.

'Nah,' said Kazza. 'My parents are up there. Disappeared.' She waved at the mountains. 'These people adopted me. To make themselves look good. That's the only reason they ever do anything. They say Circus Skills training is unsafe and undignified.'

'Well,' said Primrose. 'Off we go, out!'

'But I haven't finished recorder practice,' said Kazza, looking even gloomier than before.

'I have some news about that,' said Primrose. 'I have arranged for your recorder to be converted into a snorkel. We are going swimming with some suitable friends. At Shark Beach.'

'Wow!' said Kazza. Her face clouded. 'But isn't it dangerous?'

'Not nearly as dangerous as me,' said Primrose. 'Aw*right*!' said Kazza.

It was a pretty nice beach. The notice that said DANGER – WATER – WET burned merrily on the fire. The sea was turquoise, the sand was white, and far out near the horizon the *Kleptomanic II* rode at anchor, neat as a brochure. Better than that, everyone was there. The children of the Junta were Playing Nicely with the Lost Children.

'So,' said Cassian, stuffing a moody NO RUNNING notice into the fire. 'What happens now?'

'We've found Papa,' said Primrose, rotating a large fish on a spit over a bed of sign ashes. 'And we know the Great One's got the Chief.'

'So now we find out where this Great One is, using Papa's excellent contacts and information from the Lost Children,' said Daisy.

There was a dogged look under the film of oil on Cassian's face. 'They say they know nothing about any Great One,' he said.

There was a slight rustling in a nearby bush and the small brown figure of El Gusano appeared, picking twigs out of his hair. 'This makes us sound as if we are not heroic,' he said. 'This is not fair. Anyway in my case.'

'Cassian is an engineer, not a tactful person,' said Daisy.

'Hah!' said El Gusano, curling his lip. 'Tactful or no, this is a great insult. I shall take the Lost Children and go to the mountains, where we will live and wait for a chance to attack the Prison of the Parents.'

'But you could help down here.'

'No,' said Gusano. 'We are offended.'

'You mean sulking,' said Daisy, not too tactfully.

'We do not sulk,' said Gusano. 'We brood. Deeply, deeply we brood. And then we conquer.' He marched off down the beach.

'Twit,' said Primrose to his back. 'So that leaves Papa.'

'Sometimes,' said Daisy, 'I almost feel sorry for Papa.'

There had been sausages. Codfish sausages, with a delicious salty taste and (thought the Chief) a hint of volcano sulphur. The jigsaw puzzle was nearly finished. It was the size of a tank. Actually, it was quite like a tank in other ways. Certainly not much like a jigsaw puzzle. Definitely a machine, though the Great One said it was a jigsaw, and what the Great One said went . . .

Thinking about the Great One made the Chief's head hurt. The main thing was that the Royal Edward was very, very pleased. To have a nursery and a playroom so warm so nice plus excellent food from the vanished kingdom of Iceland was for the Chief a wonderful thing. Though of course he had not actually visited the volcano yet. Which was frustrating. The Chief found it hard to cope with frustration.

From time to time he heard the voice, so kind, so soothing.

You are happy, Your Royal Highness.

'SO HAPPY.'

People here respect you. It is niiiiiiiice to be respected.

'JA, IT IS.'

Makes a nice chaaaaaaange.

'EBSOLUTELY. EDVARD SAYS, HEV A NICE DAY.'

Stop waving your beary weary's hand, it may break off. You miss your frieeeeeeeends?

'FRIENDS? I DO NICHT . . . REMEMBER . . .'

Soooooo happy. Your friends are looooking for you. We will make them go away. Awaaaaaay. Because you are happy. Sooooooo happy . . . oooooo yes. When will the jigsaw be finished?

'JIGSAW VILL BE FINISHED VEN IT IS FINISHED. EDVARD VISHES TO SEE DER WOLKANO. UND SO DO I. VEN VILL VE SEE DER WOLKANO?'

Presently. And the keeeeeeeeeeey?

'NEVER MIND THE KEY. WOLKANO. VEN?'

Presently. First, the volcano. But more important, you will be kingy wingy. And you will be happy. Happy, happy, happeeeeeeeeeeeeeeeeeeeeeee . . .

'KINK. HEPPY. JA.'

8

That night, the fireflies on the lower slopes of the Sierra Olorosa nearly went mad. Fireflies like to get close to other fireflies. And a stream of new friends seemed to be winding doggedly through the jungle, heading steadily uphill. Except of course that the stream of fireflies was not a stream of fireflies, but the pine-resin torches of the Lost Children, El Gusano in front, tinies skipping in the middle, El Cook grumpily bringing up the rear, marching ever upward over the bad roads into the mountains. Behind and far, far below, the lights of Ciudad Olvidada glittered by the edge of the harbour.

Down there among the lights, Papa Darling was not giving a second's thought to mountains, fireflies or indeed anything except his own gigantic importance. He was arriving at a ball at the Villa Politico, dressed in tailcoat, white bow tie and very shiny black shoes. He looked about him and thought that on the whole he was too important to smile at the admiring faces on every side.

'Oo,' said Doña Amabel Deliciosa y Pronto, his partner for the evening. 'It is such an honour to be with you, Don Colin!'

'Think nothing of it, little one,' said Papa, with a small, smug smile. 'Play your cards right and you will soon become accustomed to an ongoing role as a ministerial consort.'

'Ya,' said Doña Amabel, with the slightly glazed smile of a lady who does not understand a word.

Papa Darling swept on, bowing slightly left and right. Doña Amabel's dress showed a huge amount of her top half and very little of her bottom half. Oh yes, certainly, she very much enhanced his feeling of personal significance. Show him a nature reserve, and he could have concreted it over in seconds –

He stopped.

Ahead of him, under the now-repaired chandelier, stood El Simpatico and Derek, glittering with ribbons and medals. They were flanked by the other members of the Junta. Above them on the wall was a huge picture of the nanny with the brown bowler and the pink face and the blue eyes. Papa Darling was at the very heart of government.

But there was a problem.

The problem was between smooth El Simpatico and willowy Derek. It was about waist high, pale and oval. It was a face. A small face, under a bowler hat. There was a saddle of freckles over the nose, and green eyes, which were glaring at Papa Darling. They were the eyes of his eldest child, Daisy.

Papa Darling suddenly knew what it would have felt like to be a tyre and run over a nail. He heard a voice saying, 'Gud evening, how caned, funny old weather we are having for the time of year,' and he knew the voice was his. But his mind was full of the fierce glare of those green, green eyes.

Then he was past the line and in the ballroom. 'Are you all right?' said Doña Amabel.

'All is copacetic,' said Papa Darling.

'Co wha?' said Doña Amabel. She became aware that a small nanny was standing 5 metres away, staring at her. There was something about the stare that turned Doña Amabel's knees to water. She sat down with a medium-sized crash in a little gold chair.

Papa Darling was muttering 'Excuse me' noises. Over the top of her smelling-salts bottle, Doña Amabel saw him go over and talk to the nanny.

The conversation was conducted in hisses. It went like this.

'What are you doing here?' said Papa.

'It is Primrose's night off. Where,' said Daisy, 'does the Great One live?'

'I am not at this time aware of his whereabouts,' said Papa Darling through a smile like the keys of a piano playing a sad tune.

'Then get aware,' said Daisy. 'Quickly. Or else.'

'May I remind you that I am the Minister of —'

'And may I remind you that I am your daughter?' said Daisy, smiling sweetly at her father.

Papa Darling shuddered faintly. 'Indeed,' he said. 'But I fear —'

'I have a terrible feeling,' said Daisy, taking a box from her nanny reticule, 'that something is going to go wrong with the drains. And you are Minister for Drains and Lavs, am I right?'

'Hygiene and –'

'My guess,' said Daisy, 'is that the trouble will start in the downstairs lavs.'

'Wha?' said Papa Darling.

But Daisy was gone.

He stood stupidly for a moment. Then he remembered who he had been talking to. El Simpatico and Derek liked a nice tidy house. And they liked having people to blame when things went wrong. Important people.

And Papa Darling was very, very important nowadays.

Papa Darling sprinted towards the bathroom.

He met Daisy on the way out. 'Just in time,' she said. 'Everything is in readiness.'

'Wha?' panted Papa Darling.

'Something ghastly may have happened,' she said. 'And it doesn't stop here.' Then she was gone. Papa Darling started after her.

That was when he saw the water coming under the door.

He rushed in, slammed the door behind him and wished he had not.

Reader, I will not describe the exact state of the downstairs lav at the Villa Politico. It is enough to say that the box in Daisy's hand had contained two dozen duck eggs, all rotten. Nothing in the world smells worse than a rotten duck egg. All two dozen were on the floor, broken. And someone, probably Daisy, though nothing could be proved, had shoved two pairs of football socks as far as they would go down the actual lav, then pulled the flush lever eight times.

For a moment, Papa Darling stood up to his knees in water in a fainting condition. Then he saw in the corner a mop and bucket and a pair of rubber gloves. To the handle of the mop was tied a luggage label. On the label were written the words USE ME.

Papa Darling turned purple with rage. Then he turned white with horror. Then he locked the lav door, pulled on the rubber gloves and went to work. And as he worked, his great mind battled with a great problem.

If he did what Daisy wanted and asked questions about the Great One, he would get into trouble.

But if he did not do what Daisy wanted, he would get into worse trouble. Was he more frightened of Daisy than of the Great One?

Yes. He was.

Papa Darling tried to see a Way Forward. But he could not.

So he mopped, and kept mopping.

An hour later, the lav shone brightly and smelt of flowers. Papa Darling removed the rubber gloves and straightened his white bow tie. His trousers were soaked to the knees. Still, nobody would notice. He shot the bolt, marched past the queue of angry people standing on one leg outside the door, and went looking for Doña Amabel. She had gone. 'La Doña left you a note,' said a servant, handing him an envelope.

'Ah,' said Papa Darling, opening it.

YOU ARE A HORRID HORRID DATE, NOT TO BE TRUSTED, said the note. I HOPE I NEVER SEE YOU AGAIN.

'Ahem,' said the servant.

'Wha?'

'You are dripping on the carpet,' said the servant. 'And if Your Excellency permits, there is . . . an aroma.'

'Ah,' said Papa Darling. 'Yes. I am, er, aware of the facts with regard to this one. I was just leaving.'

The ball was in full swing as he marched to the door. As he squelched out, a small figure in a brown bowler waved goodbye.

Interpersonal relationships within the family environment currently showed room for selective enhancement, thought Papa Darling.

Grrrrr.

The business at the ball had certainly been a setback, but by the next morning, after much deep breathing and several washes of his best trousers, Papa Darling had managed to take it in his stride. Now, he was dressed in a businesslike suit, and with Señora Flora Toratoratora on his arm was about to cut the first sod on the Grand Slam Dam. Papa Darling liked cutting first sods. It reminded him that soon there would be concrete everywhere. This useless little crystal stream in its useless little valley covered with useless little wild flowers would soon be blocked up with a nice grey concrete dam and full of a nice grey stagnant lake.

Papa Darling drove the spade into the ground, lifted up the bit of turf he had cut and handed it to an official. Then he mounted the steps to a stage while a man filled a glass jug with water from the stream.

'Here,' said a small nanny, materializing from the crowd. 'I'll help you with that.'

'It's all right,' said the man. But the small nanny

had rather forcefully snatched the jug away from him, and was staggering up the steps to the stage with it and plonking it on the table. The man thought that the nanny might have passed her hand over the jug and that the water in it might have turned a bit greenish.

But what could have happened to it?

Not his problem.

Papa Darling cleared his throat.

'Will it be a long speech?' said little Denis Dollar, who was there with his brother and sister and Kazza Simpatico.

'Shorter than he thinks,' said Daisy.

'And whatever you do, don't drink the water,' said Primrose.

Papa Darling began. He spoke of the wisdom of the Junta, the need for clean water, the wisdom of the Junta, the idealness of the valley, the wisdom of the Junta, the idleness of the peasants whose land was going to be flooded by the dam, and the wisdom of the Junta. He would have said more. But down there next to El Generalissimo, something was not right. What was not right were two faces, at approximately the level of El Generalissimo's shiny leather belt. The faces, one above the other, of his daughter Daisy and his daughter Primrose, watching him. Not smiling. Not scowling. Just watching, with cool eyes that saw straight through him.

Ooer.

Suddenly, all Papa Darling wanted to do was get this over and get out. He turned to the great glass jug at his side. 'Ladies and gentlemen!' he cried. 'I hereby drink the health of the Grand Slam Dam, and I hope you will join me!' He started pouring out glasses of water. Stewards handed them to the crowd. The crowd raised them high in the air. Papa Darling saw Primrose and Daisy standing there, holding up their glasses, which were sparkling in the hot Nananaguan sun. It seemed to him that there was something a little . . . *greenish* . . . about the sparkle. Unimportant, he thought. He placed the glass to his lips and swallowed the water in one dramatic gulp. Everyone else in the crowd followed suit –

No. Reader, that is an exaggeration. Everyone except two people. As Papa lowered his glass and dabbed his lips with a clean white hanky, he saw his two daughters had not lowered their glasses. They were still raised in the air. Then they turned their wrists and the water splashed on the ground in a glittering stream.

Papa Darling frowned. What, he wondered, was going on? Suddenly he felt very uneasy.

Almost immediately he felt even uneasier. Not just uneasy. Sick.

Then he was sick, all over his shoes. And through the great nastiness of being sick, he heard sounds that made him think everyone else in the crowd was being sick too.

Except Primrose and Daisy.

Everyone who had drunk the water, then.

Groo, thought Papa Darling. He straightened up. In time to see Primrose shake Daisy gravely by the hand.

Papa Darling was very, very cross. They were *naughty* children, and he would treat them that way. A good telling-off from someone as important as him would do the trick. Oh, yes. He would show them. Scowling, he marched towards his daughters. When he was halfway, someone stepped in front of him. It was Señora Flora Toratoratora. Her face was green. Diced carrots decorated her couture dress, and her eyes flashed fire. 'Poisoner!' she shrieked weakly.

'Wha?' said Papa Darling.

'You made me drink your poison water!' cried the señora. 'Enaff!' Spinning on her heel, she zigzagged huffily off between the unspeakable pools.

Papa Darling found himself looking down at two small nannies with his daughters' faces. He tried to speak. No sound came out.

'Where,' said Daisy, 'is the Great One?'

'You are not permitted to know,' said Papa Darling.

'Spit it out,' said Primrose.

'*Primrose!*' said Daisy, with what sounded like a snigger. '*Poor* Papa.'

'Poisoner!' snarled Papa Darling.

'Whoopsie Powder has no after-effects,' said Primrose.

'That's what you think,' said Papa Darling, who had now lost his patience and was trying to catch the eye of a nearby Nana.

'It is not us who is the Minister for Lavs and Clean Water,' said Daisy.

'No,' said Primrose. 'You are. And what is it that stops with you?'

Papa Darling had caught the Nana's eye. Now he went pale and did his best to avoid it. Any complaints, he realized, would reach the Great One's ears. 'With regard to my accountability in an ongoing issue of this type,' he said, 'I, er . . .'

'The buck,' said Primrose.

'Now if you will excuse us, we have children to look after,' said Daisy. 'Give us a ring when you've found out where the Great One lives. We'll be with El Simpatico.'

'Or El Generalissimo.'

'Or Señor Dollar.'

Papa Darling shuddered. What if the Great One heard?

'Yeah,' he said, and went off to find an unsicky tuft of grass on which to clean his shoes.

Next morning, Daisy spoke to Pete on the telephone. 'Listen,' she said. 'I'd like you to do some burgling in El Generalissimo's house.'

'Cor, what a relief,' said Pete. 'This child work fair does your head in after a while. Seems like years since I did a honest night's nicking. He's got medals, armour with gold on –'

'We just need a look at his diary.'

'Diary?' said Pete, disappointed. 'No spoons? Medals et cetera?'

'Diary. That's all.'

'Why?'

'We are going to make a heffalump trap and we need to find the right day.'

'Who for?' said Pete, meaning 'For whom?'

Daisy told him.

'Oh,' said Pete, sounding more cheerful. 'All *right*!'

'We'll bring the little ones to tea,' said Daisy. 'Primrose will bring the buns.'

Primrose and Daisy arrived for tea prompt at four. All three nannies leaned over the diary.

'There we are,' said Daisy. 'Junta meeting, with junior ministers –'

'– like for instance Papa –' said Primrose.

'– in the Great Hall of the People. In three days.'

'Which gives Cassian time to make a really Class A heffalump trap.'

'Lovely,' said Pete, rubbing his hands. 'We'll fix that Papa proper.'

Daisy tapped a blood-red nail thoughtfully on the tabletop. 'Yes,' she said. 'He will certainly be very keen to tell us what we need to know.' But her green eyes were troubled. Making Papa do what the little Darlings wanted was a necessary job, of course. But sometimes she thought that Pete might be taking the whole thing a little *personally*.

*

The Great Hall of the People stood at the top of an enormous flight of steps rising from the Principal Square. It was definitely Great, and definitely a Hall, but the People were not allowed in, except to a part of it walled off from the rest, in case they complained about something, which might involve throwing things at the government.

The guards on the front gate were bored. Nothing ever happened, except that occasionally all the ministers turned up for a meeting. The next meeting was in three days. Meanwhile the guards were playing cribbage.

A white van chugged round the corner and parked in front of the marble steps leading up to the marble gate. Two people in dirty white overalls got out and started taking ladders off the roof.

The smaller of the two people had a ladder in one hand, a toolbox in the other, and a very oily neck. The bigger of the two was a large and craggy person with a handle growing out of the back of his head. They went up the steps and into the Great Hall.

The hall had a golden roof held up by fat columns. In the middle of the floor stood a long table, surrounded by thirty chairs.

'Right,' said Cassian (for it was he), pulling a set

of plans from his pocket. 'Let's get to work.'

'Hur, hur,' said Luggage (for it was he), dropping his large economy-size toolboxes with a clank.

Anyone watching would have seen Cassian and Giant Luggage marching up and down the hall with forked hazel twigs in their hands, dowsing.

Dowsing?

Dowsing is using a hazel twig held in the hands to look for water. Or drainpipes. Or, in this case, sewers. The twig dips sharply when the dowser is over the top of underground water. Or drainpipes. Or, in this case, sewers.

Clear? Good.

As I was saying.

Anyone watching would have seen the hazel twigs dip sharply by a particular chair. They would have seen the toolboxes open, and a cloud of dust float up and cover the scene. From inside the cloud of dust came a whine of drills and a batter of hammers and finally a long, glutinous gurgling that spelled big, big trouble for Papa Darling –

But there was nobody watching, and nobody listening.

Which was really just as well.

*

So where is my . . . jigsaw? And my keeeeeeeeeeeeeeeeeey?

'MUST GO TO WOLKANO. YOU PROMISED.'

Sulky wulky.

'ROYAL PEOPLE DO NOT SULK. THEY ARE HAVINK OPINIONS, THIS IS ALL.'

Oooo yes. Ooooo I see. And your friends . . . have they been in touch with you?

'I AM SCHLEEPY UND SO IS EDVARD. I DO NOT REMEMBER. I VAS THINKINK YOU KNEW EVERYTHINK. MAYBE I VAS WRONG.'

Nooooo noooo. Nana knows everything. Like Nana says, soon Beobulfy Wulfy will rule a country. And Nana will be able to sail the seas in her lovely . . . that is to say, give me the keeeey, the keeeey . . .

'SCHTOP ZIS. SING ME EIN SONK. UND ALSO FOR EDVARD. MIT WOLK-ANOES IN.'

No song. No volcano. You have been bad. Now sleep. Sleeeeeeeep.

Schnore.

9

The day of the ministers' meeting dawned bright and cheery. Most days did in Nananagua; it was what came afterwards that was the problem. Papa Darling leaped out of bed in his ministerial flat, sprang out of his pyjamas and cast himself into a cold shower. All through breakfast he dictated memos to Señorita Rita Pumkinita, his secretary. Señorita Pumkinita kept her flashing eyes on the page, but Papa could tell she was beginning to admire him greatly. His thoughts strayed for a moment to a woman of supreme elegance, sitting at a piano. He saw himself standing by that piano. He was singing 'Stand by Me' with the woman, and three little faces were watching through the banisters. He became aware that he was saying something, he could not tell what . . .

He shuddered and wrenched his thoughts back to the present. Señorita Pumkinita was staring at him with her mouth open. He said, 'With regard to my remarks heretofore, er, I seem to have mislaid the, er, thread –'

'You were saying,' said Señorita Pumkinita, lowering her hugely mascaraed eyelids and reading from her pad, '"O horror of horrors it is happening all over again I am walking blindfold into a quagmire."'

'Heh heh,' said Papa Darling in a hollow voice. 'Just my little humorous remark or joke.'

'Heh heh,' said Señorita Pumkinita, with the smallest of smiles. It had not been funny, and besides she did not want to crack her lipstick.

'Finish it off, yours sincerely, all that. Well, can't sit here, er, joking all morning,' said Papa Darling. He scooped up his briefcase, snapped open his phone and clattered down the front steps to his car.

The picture of the piano and the children was fading in his mind. Oh, yes, he told himself. The past was so *last week*. Colin Darling was on his way again.

Juntas were all very well. But Nananagua was a nice little country. Hot, dirty, true. But pleasant beaches. Crying out for a coating of concrete, a thriving tourist trade. And a man to run it. A man not afraid to take tough decisions.

Papa Darling's lips moved. 'El Presidente Colin Darling,' he said to himself.

It definitely had that ring.

And once the people heard the speech he had typed out and put in his briefcase, he would be unstoppable.

The limousine purred through Ciudad Olvidada. There was a crowd on the steps in front of the Great Hall of the People. The car stopped. The crowd cheered at gunpoint. A small person stepped forward, bowed deeply and said, 'Carry your briefcase, O great and noble minister?' Papa Darling handed over the briefcase without a thought, happy to have both hands free for waving.

Then he noticed the neck of the small person who had taken his briefcase. The neck on which there were undoubted stains of engine oil. Of the kind that generally appeared on the neck of his son, Cassian. Whom, come to think of it, the small person closely resembled. Though it was hard to check, because he had vanished into the crowd.

Papa Darling's heart froze in his chest as he climbed the steps. What if his briefcase and the speech inside it got stolen?

But there at the top of the steps was a smiling guard, holding out the briefcase.

Papa Darling's heart became as warm and comforting as a roast chestnut. He waved and smiled and took the briefcase from the guard and stalked into the conference chamber of the Great Hall of the People, stealing as he went a glance at the lock on the case. He was reassured. There had been no tampering. Only a very, very clever locksmith could possibly get in there. And there were no locksmiths that clever in Nananagua.

Except (and this thought never entered Papa Darling's very big head) his son, Cassian.

Papa Darling strode to the table. He placed the case in front of his chair. The Public Gallery was full.

There was a flourish of trumpets.

The Junta came in. From her picture on the wall,

the nanny with the pink face and the ghastly blue eyes looked down.

El Simpatico made a speech introducing Papa Darling. Papa Darling twirled the combination lock of his briefcase and took out his sheaf of notes.

'And now I hand you over to a new colleague,' said El Simpatico. 'Dedicated to a clean, *safe* Nananagua. Señor El Minister Colin Darling!'

There were murmurs of 'Hear, hear!' and 'Who?'

Papa Darling fixed a grave, responsible expression to his face and stood up.

'Junta, ladies and gentlemen,' he said. Then he looked down at his notes.

Or what he had thought were his notes.

Which did not seem to be his notes any more.

Papa Darling's notes had been neatly typed in three colours. The papers between his fingers bore writing in thick black pen, apparently done by someone using both hands.

ASK THEM WHERE THE GRATE ONE IS, said the note. IF YOU DO NOT DO THIS NOW THIS MINIT THE CHAIR OF EL SIMPATTICOE WILL FALL THROUGH THE FLOOR AND INTO A DRANE. AND YOU WILL BE BLAIMED. Instead of a signature there was an oily black thumbprint.

In the Public Gallery, the small person with dark hair and oil smudges on his face was definitely his son, Cassian. And definitely waving.

Papa Darling looked down and turned to the next page. WE MEEN IT, said the writing, in red ink this time. Or was it blood? DO IT NOW.

'Ahem,' said El Simpatico.

Papa Darling realized that he had been looking at his notes for a very long time. He gulped.

Cassian was now gazing at him with his finger poised over . . . *a remote control*. Giant Luggage was beside him, grinning. Oh noooo, thought Papa Darling. 'But first,' said Papa Darling hastily, 'I have received a humble, well, a fairly humble petition from a citizen. We all admire the Great One. So, ah, why can we not know where this great personage lives? So we can bring this great personage, er, thanks and praise?'

There was a silence. El Simpatico's eyebrows had crawled up his forehead. El Generalissimo's neck bulge had turned scarlet. Señor Dollar was scowling horribly at his calculator.

Papa Darling sat down suddenly.

El Simpatico spoke in his high, chilly, reasonable voice. 'Because we are not worthy. The Great One must be a mystery.' His eyes travelled to the nanny portrait on the wall. 'Above all at times like now, when there are Great Events in the air. Bless the Great One.'

'Bless the Great One,' muttered all present, many with their fingers crossed.

El Simpatico's eyes returned to Papa Darling like homing marbles. 'Nanas!' he barked. Papa Darling sat like a rabbit in the headlights. 'The Cell of Death, I think,' said El Simpatico mildly.

The Nanas on either side of the door marched towards Papa Darling. One took his left arm. The other took his right arm. They pulled him out of his chair like a cork out of a bottle and carried him towards a small iron door in the far wall.

'Cassian!' howled Papa Darling, pedalling feebly.

Whoops, thought Cassian. His plan had been to get information, not an arrested father. He was a bit unclear about what to do next. Well, he thought, when in doubt, do something mechanical. His finger came down on the remote control.

One moment El Simpatico was sitting in his chair. The next there was no El Simpatico and no chair, only a dull rumble, a square black hole in the white marble floor and a thin, fading 'AIEEEEE'. Then a splash, a gurgle, and silence.

For a second.

Then there was a lot of noise.

A huge voice was bellowing, 'CLEAR THE HALL!' The public began to pile out. Beyond the bombproof glass separating the public from the conference chamber, a specialist unit of skindivers was clustering round the hole in the floor, while firemen trundled in a small crane. As Cassian shuffled along in the slow queue to the exit, he was privileged to see El Simpatico winched dripping from the hole.

'He's hurt!' said someone in the queue.

'Hope it's something serious,' said someone else.

'Sssh,' said someone else. They were at the exit, and four giant Nanas were searching everyone.

'Oops,' said a small man, going a nasty grey colour. 'Them's the Great One's personal bodyguards.'

Beady eyes examined Cassian's personal toolkit and bag of boiled sweets. The toolkit came back, but not the sweets. That was Nanas for you. Readjusting his rumpled clothes, he walked into the bright sunlight and waited for Luggage.

Luggage did not come.

Under pretence of seeking shade, Cassian shuffled back along the wall until he could see the searching

Nanas. Luggage was standing nose to nose with the biggest of them. Cassian made himself extra small. It looked as if they were arm-wrestling. Luggage might laugh a lot – actually, he did nothing else – but he was a mighty arm-wrestler. Someone was going to get hurt.

Luggage was Cassian's friend. He could not leave him. But he could not stick around either. There were Nanas everywhere. He had a dry mouth and the unusual feeling that while he was certainly a mechanical genius, he was only eleven years old.

He scowled until his thick black hair met his thick black eyebrows, and thought until his ears got hot. And as he thought, he realized things.

He had seen the Nana opposite Luggage before: that low forehead, those huge scarred knuckles. She was Nanny Dangerfield, the Flying Nanny. The very important Flying Nanny, who was known to be close to the Great One. And who had fancied Luggage. Now she and Luggage were standing nose to nose. Arm-wrestling . . .

Hold on, thought the Cassian that had been educated by two strong-minded sisters. This was not your simple arm-wrestling.

Luggage and the Flying Nanny were standing nose

to nose staring deep into each other's eyes . . . *holding hands*.

Yeuuch! thought Cassian. Eurgghh! *Revolting!*

Drifting into the shade, he sat down and concentrated on hanging around.

They held hands for ten minutes by his watch. Then they strolled down to the seaside, still holding hands. Cassian went after them. He was astonished to see them stroll through a lot of very interesting scrap metal without apparently even noticing it. At last, the Nana looked at the heavy steel watch pinned to her dress. She said something to Luggage and punched him hard but affectionately on the jaw. Luggage thumped her lovingly back on the nose. With a twinkle of her mighty brogues, she was gone.

'Hur, hur,' said Luggage, standing in a romantic trance by the wreckage of a sludge gulper. Then, 'Hur?'

For Cassian had materialized by his right knee.

'That Nana is one of the Great One's head bodyguards,' said Cassian. 'She will lead us to the Great One. Follow her. Go where she goes. Then come back and report. Forget, er, love. This is war.' He examined Luggage closely, looking for signs of intelligence and seeing none.

Luggage frowned. 'Hur,' he said. Then the handle on the back of his head moved up and down. He seemed to be nodding. His huge, craggy face split into a landslide of a grin. 'HUR!' he cried. And off he went, galumphing in the broguesteps of his beloved.

Cassian walked slowly on his way. He had never suspected Luggage of bendy thinking, and it came as a shock. It was time for a conference with those members of his family who were not yet in jail.

The Captain leaned against the wheel of the *Kleptomanic II*, one perfect mauve shoe massaging the teak floorboards, and surveyed Daisy, Primrose, Cassian and Pete, who were on their day off. 'So,' she said. 'The situation is this. Papa Darling has been hauled off to the Caboose following the failure of your clever scheme to make him confess all, Cassian. Goodness knows what they will do to him in there. Does one care?' She swept the wheelhouse with a glance from under her endless lashes, and sighed, 'I suppose in the end one does. In the same way that one might be kind to a stray —'

'Dog,' said Pete.

'I was going to say stranger on a train,' said the Captain mildly. 'Now, reports, please, everyone.'

'The Chief slept at El Generalissimo's,' said Pete. 'I seen his toothmarks on the bed.'

'And he had coffee at the Dollars',' said Daisy. 'I saw toothmarks on the coffee table, so he was obviously happy.'

'And he had a sit-down on a throne at El Simpatico and Derek's,' said Primrose. 'I saw his toothmarks on a throne, with a brass plaque.'

'It is almost,' said the Captain, 'as if he was introduced to the Junta one by one, getting steadily happier, and was then spirited away by this Great One. What can be going on?'

'You can bet Papa knows,' said Cassian.

'But Papa is in jail,' said the Captain. 'Think what happened last time you went there.'

'Ho!' cried a tiny voice, and all in the room turned to see Nosey Clanger peering over the top of the Captain's Prada handbag. 'Lemme at 'em! I'll releaf the prifonerf, find the Chief, let out Papa, pluff I'll fpifflicate the lot of 'em. I'll –'

'I'm sure you will,' said the Captain kindly. 'But for now, the sun will be going down, and you have had a busy week, and it is your night off. A night in the nick will do Papa no harm. I think we should relax and wait till the morning.'

The evening started with a supper of minestrone soup, roast beef and six veg, strawberry and Guernsey cream double bombe Pavlova Elysium. Then there was community singing and stunt burgling. The high spot came when Sophie Nickit demonstrated her legendary Underpants Removal Without Disturbance to Outer Garments, using Pete as her victim.

Though Pete laughed heartily as the petite lady burglar waved his Y-fronts in the air, the evening as a whole was a little subdued. The *Kleptomanic*'s crew were a team, and they wanted their members back, however odd. So everyone went to bed a little early and slept extremely well.

Unlike, dear reader, the missing members. Who for the record were occupied as follows:

1. *Papa Darling*. Locked in the Cell of Death, a small dungeon hewn out of the living rock. The door was overhead, more like a trapdoor than a door. For company he had several newts, something that might by the sound of it have been a rattlesnake, and many inscriptions on the cell walls. The bad thing about

the inscriptions was that they all seemed to be last wills and testaments, scratched in the rock by people who were about to face ghastly fates. The good thing about the inscriptions was that they were very deeply carved, which in rock of this hardness meant that they had taken a long time to do, which meant that their writers had probably spent some years there before the ghastly fates had kicked in. This was not an absolutely amazingly brilliant thing, of course. But it was the only thing Papa Darling could see that even vaguely resembled an upside.

Because the candle that was his only light had one centimetre left to burn. And the cell was rather damp. And getting damper.

2. *Giant Luggage.* Crouched behind a boulder on a steep mountainside overlooking a valley. The valley was guarded by a high and dangerous fence and carpeted with beautiful green grass, on which stood tidy little cottages, each with a veranda. On the verandas, nannies were sitting round tables with neat gingham cloths, playing cribbage and drinking gin.

Luggage had run up into the mountains hand in hand with Nanny Dangerfield and clouted her a loving goodbye at the gate of the nanny camp. Then he had come up to this steep and hidden spot because (as far as anyone could tell) he was feeling lonely and wished to brood, and watch, of course. From his eyrie he had seen a strange sight.

Instead of joining one of the little groups on the cottage verandas, Nanny Dangerfield had walked up to the blind end of the valley. The final 50 metres of the valley narrowed to a ravine that ended in a wall of living rock. In the middle of the wall was a neat door, painted beige. In the middle of the door was a brightly polished brass bell. Nanny Dangerfield had walked down the ravine and pressed the bell. The door had opened. Light had streamed out. Two large nanny guards had surrounded her. There had been a password and a response. The nanny guards had let Nanny Dangerfield in. She had not come out.

Luggage seemed to think for a bit (though of course it was impossible to tell if he was thinking or not). Then, fluttering his salami-sized fingers sentimentally at the beige door, he began to clump back down the mountain towards the coast.

3. *Chief Engineer Crown Prince Beowulf of Iceland (deposed), B.Eng. (Reykjavik).* Happiness. Warm, pink

happiness. The smell of the Royal Edward, faintly tinged with sulphur. A rocking movement. A voice with a lullaby:

Rockington Rockington Rockington Ree,
O what a very good Crown Prince is Ye.
When you got a minute, give us the key.

Suck thumb.
  Happy, happy, happy.

10

The sun came out of the sea like a well-kicked football. In the green trees across the blue water, ten thousand birds started singing. In the State Suite of the *Kleptomanic II*, where she was sleeping away the last of her 24 hours off, Daisy's eyes slammed open.

Something was clanging on the hull.

Pulling on an attractive suit of green silk deck pyjamas, she ran briskly up the companionway. Her brother and sister came too. The clanging was louder up here, and there was a knot of burglars gathered by the railings on the port side. Standing on tiptoe, she peered over the rail.

Far below, a mighty figure was treading water and battering the hull with fists like sledgehammers.

'Mind my paint!' shrieked Lars Chance, the Sailing Master.

'Never mind your paint, and anyway it's ours now,' said Daisy. 'Someone lower something or something.'

A hook was lowered. It caught the handle at the back of Luggage's head, hauled him dripping from the sea and placed him on the deck.

'Well?' said Cassian.

'Hur, hur,' said Giant Luggage and pointed a mighty finger at the green mountains inland.

'Dumbo,' said Primrose.

'Ssh,' said Cassian, frowning. For Giant Luggage was making various expressive gestures with his enormous hands.

'What's he waving his arms for?' said Primrose.

'He is saying,' said Cassian, 'that he followed his beloved to the Valley of the Nannies, that there are between 411 and 413 nannies there, but that the defences are daunting, featuring entanglements of size-14 razor wire, 30,000,000-volt electrified strand, fields of type-31 mines and a guard dog, half Alsatian, half Pomeranian. He is saying that it is hard to be sure why the nannies are living there, but that there is obviously something of great importance behind a beige door in a sandstone cliff at the head of the valley. There is no sign of the Lost Children, so presumably they have given up on the Great One and are watching their parents, who are in a prison camp nearby.'

'Is that all?' said Daisy.

'He says he is sorry not to be more precise.'

'I should think so too,' said Daisy. 'So I expect you will be heading for the hills, Cassian?'

'Yep,' said Cassian. 'This Vallenana sounds very promising. I shall go up there and keep watch. Luggage can be my messenger.'

'And Primrose, Pete and I will be picking up our charges and heading for an educational visit to the Caboose, for Papa, obviously, and,' said Daisy, meditatively, 'it might be useful to have a word with the Junta's old nannies. Captain, if I could recruit a small elite burglary squad?'

'Naturally.'

'*Thank* you.' Climbing on to a lifeboat, Daisy

cleared her throat. 'I need two precision burglars for an errand of some difficulty. Hands up?'

Sophie Nickit raised a hand. Fingers McMurtrie did not raise his, but he leaped a foot in the air, because Nosey Clanger had raised his, and it had caught Fingers McMurtrie in a painful spot.

'Excellent,' said Daisy. 'The crème de la crème. Now. Is everybody ready?'

Everybody was.

'Off we go,' said Daisy.

There were extra guards reinforcing the Nanas at the front door of the Caboose since the tunnel scandal. The Great One did not like people escaping, and what the Great One did not like the Great One did not get. The extra guards were tough ones. So the Nanas had left it to them.

Fat Enrico was the toughest guard of the lot, and he was feeling particularly tough that day. His breakfast live chicken had not gone down at all well and he wanted some rum to drown it with. But the Nanas had said no rum while you are on duty, Fat Enrico. So Enrico was in a foul mood.

This mood was not improved by the procession heading up the Street of the Doomed in his general direction. There seemed to be five nannies and six children. Fat Enrico had nothing against children, raw or cooked. But he had had a bellyful of Nanas. Ever since there had been Nanas in Nananagua the place had gone to the dogs.

The nannies arrived at the gate. 'G'morning, my good man,' said the lead nanny, who had brilliant green eyes and perfect nail varnish. 'We have come to visit our colleagues kept in durance vile.'

'Where's that?' said Enrico.

'Captivity, moron. Open up, chop, chop,' said a slightly smaller nanny with mild blue eyes and pale yellow hair.

'Or I'll fpifflicate –'

'It would be *so* kind,' said a rather pretty nanny, pushing the absolutely tiny toothless nanny behind her.

'No,' said Enrico.

'Please?' said the pretty nanny, who was Sophie Nickit, obviously. She patted him on the arm.

'No,' said Enrico, who had actually quite liked being patted.

'Poor you. Have you by any chance got indigestion?' said the blonde nanny.

Enrico was amazed. 'Cor,' he said. 'Psychic. It

gets me just under the right-hand ribs, like.'

The blonde nanny held out a tin of large white sweets. 'Try one of these,' she said. 'You will find them soothing.'

Enrico snarled at her and grabbed a rude handful. He stuffed them in his mouth and crunched revoltingly.

'Timberr,' said Primrose, for it was she.

Enrico hit the ground, which shook.

'Knock-Out Drops?' said Daisy.

'Concussion Creams,' said Primrose. 'Same thing, but hits you harder.'

The pretty nanny who was Sophie Nickit was unlocking the huge nailed door with the keys she had removed from Enrico's belt while she had been patting his arm. The nannies and their charges strolled into the slimy interior of the Caboose.

'Wha?' said a guard inside the door. Then he saw the nanny uniforms, turned white and began to shudder a lot.

Pete said, 'We have come to visit –'

'Interrogate,' said Daisy.

'– like she said, question and torture horribly the nannies you are holding. And look at the Cell of Death. While these children watch.'

'It will be educational,' said Daisy.

'Aye, aye,' said the guard, sheets of sweat sliding down his face. 'Cell of Death, downstairs. The nannies is in the Topmost Turret, innit?'

'Topmost Turret it is. Ta very much.'

'Don't mench.'

'Forward!' cried Daisy.

'Yeah,' said Pete. 'Now, kids. This is a prison, and a nasty one. On yer left, steps down to where they keep people in horrid dank cells, like for instance me last week. Straight ahead, the way to the Topmost Turret, which is drier but draughtier.'

'I don't like it,' said Kazza, lip trembling.

'Nor do we,' said Stalin and Napoleon and the Dollar children.

'Nobody does,' said Sophie Nickit. 'We'll scout around in the lower regions. Catch you later?'

'Ice,' said Pete.

'Sorry?'

'Ice cream, cool as a mountain stream.'

'Ah.'

'Pete,' said Daisy, 'that is absolutely enough bad rhyming slang, plus I have noticed that you only do it when you are nervous. Now, children. On we go. At home, we are told that the purpose of prison is to punish people who are bad, while teaching them to be good. In Nananagua, the purpose of prison is to keep people locked up until the cows come home, i.e., forever.'

'Here we are,' said Pete.

They were outside a mighty wooden door studded with iron nails and anchored with heavy bolts and hinges.

'Hush!' said Daisy, raising a scarlet-nailed forefinger.

From inside came a curious clinking noise.

'Teacups,' said Daisy. 'Right. Little ones, you go and play in the torture chamber, first on the left. Nannies, in we go.'

It was a domed room of mouldy stone, with a stone floor and curtains with bunny rabbits on them. In the middle of the floor was a grubby wooden table with splintery benches round it. On the table were a teapot and several cups. On the benches sat nannies. Their uniforms were frankly grubby, their brogues stained with prison filth. They were talking the usual nanny drivel.

'It's a long lane that has no turning,' said one of them.

'There's many a slip between cup and lip,' said another.

'Many hands make light work,' said another.

'Ahem,' said Daisy.

They looked round slowly. Their eyes had a blank, mad stare.

'Sorry to see you all in this state,' said Daisy insincerely.

'It's scandalous,' said Nanny Clam.

'Disgusting,' said Nanny Potter.

'None too hygienic,' said Nanny Divine.

'Sorry you don't like it,' said Daisy, with extreme cruelty. 'Particularly because you are in here forever.'

The dull eyes rested on her like prunes.

'Unless –' said Daisy.

The three pairs of eyes blinked like one pair of eyes.

'Unless you tell me everything.'

'Everything?'

'Everything,' said Primrose.

'Number one,' said Daisy. 'What are three ancient-type nannies doing in a hot filthy spot like Nananagua?'

'The rich people want their children looked after.'

'Possibly,' said Daisy. 'But one feels there is more to it than that. What we need is a spokesnanny. Nanny Potter?'

'My lips are sealed,' said Nanny Potter.

'Then you will never get out of prison. Nanny Clam?'

'I cannot betray a confidence.'

'Then Nanny Potter will have company. Nanny Divine?'

'I will tell everything!' blubbered Nanny Divine, cracking like an egg.

'Wretch!' hissed Nanny Potter.

'Traitor!' hissed Nanny Clam.

'It's no good! It's the way Nanny Potter sniffs, and the way Nanny Clam pulls hairs out of her chin with her fingernails, and the shame of being nannies locked up for bad behaviour by other nannies. You can really get me out?'

'One good turn deserves another,' said Primrose.

'All right. I was working for the Duchess of Mountratchet, two children, charming but pale, when I got a letter that said did I want an all-expenses-paid career in the sun, absolute control of household, high salary, muted beige Honda Aerodeck? So of course I leaped at the chance and I know the other nannies did too.'

'Anyone would,' said Nanny Potter.

'Sneak,' said Nanny Clam.

'And who wrote the letter?'

'One who cannot be named.'

'And what was this person called?'

'Nanny –'

'Grass!' hissed Potter.

'Nanny –'

'Peach!'

'Nanny –'

'Goodbye,' said Daisy, and started for the door.

'NANNY DESTINY!' yelled all three nannies at once in most unladylike voices.

There was a great and bottomless silence. Daisy and Primrose stared at each other. They were thinking of the pink nanny portraits in the nurseries and government offices and bars and just about everywhere else in Nananagua. How could they have been so blind?

Daisy pulled herself together. 'Nanny Destiny, otherwise known as the Great One?' she said.

The nannies nodded.

'So you choose freedom,' said Daisy.

The nannies' faces were buried in their big hard hands. 'Yiss,' they sobbed. 'We do, we do.'

'There, there, Nannies,' said Daisy. 'So why don't you tell me all about it?'

'Where do we start?'

'At the beginning,' said Daisy. 'Continuing to the end.'

'If we are named as sneaks, the results will be awful.'

'We will turn our backs,' said Daisy. 'And you may put cushions over your heads. Nobody will know who is speaking.'

'Oo,' said the Nannies, and there was hope in their silly old voices.

Daisy, Primrose and Nanny Pete turned round. There was muttering as the nannies drew straws for who was going to be the one to confess.

'Ready?' said a voice, gloomy but muffled, as if speaking through a cushion.

'We do not recognize your voice,' said Daisy. 'Go ahead, Nanny X.'

'So we came out here,' said Nanny X, who actually sounded much like Nanny Potter with her head in a cushion cover. 'And we found Nanny Destiny, who had been marooned from a luxury yacht, looking after the children of El Presidente Real Banana. But El Presidente and his lady turned out to be weak people with bad views on bringing up children. They read the children stories –'

'Tch.'

'– and took them on walks –'

'Tch, *tch*.'

'– and to the beach. So they were independent little brutes, with their own thoughts and their own ponies. Naturally Nanny Destiny could not be expected to put up with this. There was a clash of wills. Obviously Nanny Destiny won. She is a remarkable woman, a truly elite nanny who has worked in the front line, i.e., for royalty. El Presidente and his parliament went first into hiding and then, when Nanny Destiny found them, into a camp in the hills. Their children were of course taken away from them. Nanny Destiny started a police force of locally trained nannies –'

'Las Nanas?' said Pete.

'Exactly. The sweepings of the jails, but very talented in their way. Anyway. Nanny Destiny spent a short time running the country. It used to be called the Volcano Coast. She changed its name to Nananagua, made a lot of very sensible laws so nobody would hurt themselves or think unsuitable thoughts, and found some tidy people to be ever such a nice Junta. And of course the Junta needed people to look after their children and the locals were too, too rough, so she put advertisements in the *Nanny Gazette* –'

'In her wisdom –' said another disguised voice.

'Her great, *great* wisdom –' said a third voice, so heavily disguised it sounded like a pig grunting.

'– and we answered. Bringing with us, I may say, the highest references. And here we are. Or were. Doing very, very nicely. Until, well . . .'

'Until we came along,' said Daisy. 'And gave you what you richly deserved.'

'Well!' said a muffled nanny.

'The *idea*!' said another.

'Wash your mouth out with soap and –'

'Stop!' cried Daisy in a voice like a whip cracking. 'Tell me. Where is this Nanny Distemper –'

'Destiny.'

'– whatever, now?'

'In her beige sitting room.'

Daisy's brogue started tapping danger signals on the slimy stones. 'Where is this sitting room?'

'We do not know.'

'All we know,' said Nanny Clam's cushion cover, 'is that one hears . . . from one's highly placed sources, of course . . . that she now has a little charge *worthy of her past experience*.'

'Wha?' said Primrose.

'Wha?' said Pete.

'She means that this Great One has got someone royal to look after,' said Daisy. 'Obviously.'

The three nannies started to make noises like a loftful of pigeons: Oo coo that's what you think, hoo we knoo better than you –

And stopped. Well, they did not exactly stop. Reader, the dash at the end of the last paragraph is where Daisy, having pushed Pete and Primrose into the corridor, slammed the door and double-locked it.

'We've got the Chief,' said Daisy. 'As good as.'

'Wha?'

'This Nanny Dustbin –'

'Destiny.'

'– whatever, has a beige sitting room. Luggage saw one of the Great One's top bodyguards go into a beige door in a heavily guarded cliff. What does that mean to you?'

'It means we should check with Papa and get up there.'

Down the stairs they went. They met several guards, all of whom stood closely back against the walls and saluted the uniforms. Must be quite a nanny, this Disintegration.

Destiny.

Whatever.

Daisy was rather looking forward to meeting her.

While the Darling girls and Pete had been reasoning with the nannies in the Topmost Turret, Papa Darling had been having a rather trying time in the Cell of Death. The cell had got damper and damper, and was now half full of water. The light had gone out. It was very dark. It was unpleasantly obvious to Papa that the water in the cell was rising. It was pushing him on to the only bit of dry ground, which was alarmingly close to the roof and was already occupied by the thing he had thought was a rattlesnake, which he was now almost sure was a rattlesnake, and a rather cross one at that.

Now, Papa Darling was standing up to his nostrils in cold, dirty water, and wishing he had led a better life, or at any rate that El Simpatico had not fallen through the hole in the floor of the Great Hall of the People and landed in a sewer.

'Psst,' said a voice from the direction of the door.

Papa Darling assumed it was another snake. He resigned himself to a frightful end.

'Oi,' said the voice. 'You comin' out?'

Snakes may hiss, but they do not say 'Oi'.

So Papa Darling said, 'Yes.' Or meant to. But his mouth was underwater, so what came out was blblblblblb.

He waited. There was a scratching from the door and a rattle from the snake. The water rose a bit more, so he had to stand on tiptoe to breathe. Then the trapdoor opened, and Papa Darling put up his arms and hauled himself into the brilliant light of . . .

Actually, what he hauled himself into was a rather nasty passage, lit by a guttering orange oil lamp. But it looked pretty bright to him, and reader, just at the moment we are seeing things through Papa Darling's eyes.

So he sat there and dripped a bit. As his vision cleared, he saw two nannies facing him. One of them came up to his knee, and wore (besides the uniform) many tattoos and an expression of raw savagery. The other was a very pretty nanny indeed.

'Rattlesnakes,' croaked Papa Darling, pointing at the cell.

Instantly the tiny nanny leaped into the Cell of Death. Sounds of sloshing and grunts of effort came from the darkness, followed by a long, despairing rattle. Nosey reappeared, holding the twisting reptile by the neck. 'Big 'un,' he said. 'I fort of fpifflicaped 'im.'

'Urgh,' said Papa Darling.

'Excellent companion, a fnake,' said Nosey. 'You know where you are wif a rappler. Or anyway you know where the rappler if. Becaufe of the rapple.'

'Now if you have quite finished your nature-study lecture,' said Sophie Nickit, 'there is, um . . .'

Down the passage came a large guard. ''Ello 'ello, what's all this then?' he cried, twirling his moustache and looking Sophie up and down.

''Ello 'ello,' said Sophie, winking and sidling up to him.

The guard was very pleased when the pretty lady hugged him. It was always nice when prisoners hugged you before you put them in the Cell of Death. Then the pretty lady stepped back. She was holding something up. The guard frowned. He seemed to recognize it. In fact he definitely recognized it. His braces, for a start. And his belt. At this point his trousers fell down. 'Aiee!' he cried, turning modestly to the wall.

'Have your belp bap,' said the tiny nanny.

The guard groped behind him and took the long thin thing that the tiny nanny was offering him. He had it through two loops before he realized that the thing he was threading was not a belt but a rattlesnake. A rattlesnake that had been in a bad mood to start with and whose mood had been going downhill ever since.

'Aiee!' cried the guard again.

Papa Darling, Sophie Nickit and Nosey looked back as they reached the corner in the passage. Reader, it is never easy to try to run away from your trousers when you are wearing them. The guard was doing his best, but it looked as if his best would not be good enough.

'Off we go!' cried Sophie Nickit.

Off they went. They met Primrose, Daisy and Pete coming down the passage. 'All right,' said Daisy. 'We know all. We want a full account of exactly what is going on with Nanny Dinnergong –'

'Destiny –'

'Whatever, and the Chief, and the Junta, and all the rest of it. Well?'

'I don't know –'

'Or it's the dungeon again.'

'All right,' said Papa Darling. 'The Junta are going to be made into dukes. I was going to be made into a noble count.'

'Why?'

'Because the Chief is going to be crowned King of Nananagua. He needs a court.'

'It will never happen,' said Daisy.

'Trust us on this,' said Primrose. 'Your choice is, prison or the ship?'

'Ahem,' said Papa. 'I feel that the seafaring life is both free and offers many opportunities –'

'Lower-deck lavs it is,' said Primrose. 'With extra handcuffs.'

'Believe me,' said Papa earnestly, 'handcuffs will not be necessary. I have taken on board this situation –'

'Wha?' said his daughter.

'– that is to say, learned my lesson.'

'Good.'

They walked down to the docks. Primrose held one of Papa's hands. Daisy held the other. It was nice to be two girls of twelve and a bit and ten and a bit, walking through a rather nasty city holding hands with their daddy. And there was another thing they knew instinctively in their Darling hearts. Which was that unless they hung on to him, he might easily run away.

As they walked across the quay several policemen started towards them, then veered hastily away when they saw the telltale bowler hats.

'What's that?' said Primrose suddenly.

She was pointing at a bump on top of the steps where the *Kleptomanic* had been tied up.

'Luggage!' cried Daisy. 'Back from the mountains!'

'Hur,' said Luggage, holding out his hand. In it was a folded paper, slightly smeared with oil.

'A note,' said Primrose, stating the obvious.

'From Cassian,' said Daisy, doing the same.

'Is somebody going to read it?' said Pete.

Daisy held the note in front of her. She cleared her throat and squinted at the writing, thick and black in the glow of a handy quay light. 'It says here,' she read, '"Intresting develipmants. Wil be at El Arble dell Morto every daie at none. The Crisis Aprooches. Com sone."'

'I'll arrange a bus,' said Pete. 'You bring the snax.'

Off they all went.

It was all sleepy-byes now. But sometimes the Chief dreamed.

He dreamed he was making the jigsaw, except he called it the yigsaw, and that the Royal Edward was standing on the workbench giving him advice. The Royal Edward had a paw in the air. 'Why are you making this thing that looks like a machine not a jigsaw?' the Royal Edward was saying.

'Because She tells me to,' said the Chief, in a voice that was the voice of an extremely young person. 'And She says that ven I have finish She vill make me kink.'

'Tells?' said the Royal Edward. 'Your Royal Highness, "tells" is not what someone who is basically a member of staff does to His Royal Highness Crown Prince Beowulf.'

'All right, all right,' said the Chief in his dream.

'Ja,' said the Royal Edward. '"Humbly begs" is what a member of staff does.'

'It is Her eyes,' said the Chief.

'Eyes, schmeyes,' said the Royal Edward.

'UND HOW VOULD YOU KNOW ABOUT EYES,' cried the Chief in his dream. 'YOU WHO HAVE SCHUPID BLEK BUTTONS INSTEAD. END ARE FULL OF SCHUPID SAWDUST.'

'Yiss,' said the Royal Edward, obviously deeply

offended. 'One may be made of sawdust, but one has a proud heart.'

'NOOOO!' cried the Chief. 'I HAVE OFFENDED HIM! IT IS BECAUSE OF NO WOLKANO!' He woke shouting.

To find the Eyes looking at him.

Back to wooooork, said the voice. *Then I will make you king, and you will give me the keeeeeeeeeeeey?*

'WOLKANO FIRST,' howled the Chief, clasping the Edward to his bosom.

Back to sleeeeeeeeeep, said the voice. *Sleeeeeeeeep.*

Schnore.

11

The minibus buzzed merrily into the mountains. Pete was driving.

'Yuk!' cried the Dollar children, who in the joy of freedom had changed their names to Horko, Yorko and Beans. 'What is that?'

'A tree,' said Primrose.

The minibus was travelling across a wide, flat valley, floored with yellowish grass through which the red earth showed. The sky was full of thunderclouds. Between the clouds were patches of blue sky in which wheeled little black dots.

'Vultures,' said Daisy.

The tree stood in the middle of the valley. It was huge and dark, with a clotted look. As the minibus drew near it, the clots on its branches spread their wings and flapped heavily into the sky.

'The Arble dell Morto means Arbol del Muerto. Arbol del Muerto means Dead Man's Tree,' said Primrose, largely, dear reader, for your benefit.

The children were losing their splendid new-found confidence and showed signs of grizzling.

'Look!' cried Primrose. 'Here comes Cassian!'

And sure enough, from under the tree was walking the small, dark and oil-stained figure of their brother. 'Hello,' he said to his sisters. 'Got any lunch?'

'Obviously,' said Primrose.

It was an excellent lunch, with four different kinds of pie (steak, steak and kidney, chicken, vegetarian samosa) and many exotic salads, including Greek.

'Phew!' said Pete, wiping his mouth. 'OK, saucepans. What now?'

'Map time,' said Cassian, spreading a sheet of fairly oily paper in the dust. 'Here is the Camp of the Children. On the other side of the mountain is the Prison of the Parents. And up here, Vallenana, the Valley of Los Bungalos Guarding the Beige Door. So in we get, and I'll drive you to the children!'

'No way,' said Pete. 'I drive.'

'Spose,' said Cassian.

Off they went.

The Camp of the Children was a masterpiece of camouflage. The houses looked like piles of stone, which in fact they were. The seats looked like fallen trees, which in fact they were. The children came out of their holes and sang a song of welcome:

> *Welcome, lovely Daisy!*
> *It's for you this song is sang.*
> *Welcome Primrose and your food!*
> *Say goodbye to hunger's pang!*
> *Welcome also Nanny Pete!*
> *Say hello to rhyming slang!*
> *Me old china.*
> *Wha?*
> *China plate,*
> *Mate.*

'Nice one,' said Pete, blushing slightly.

It had certainly been an amazing transformation.

The Lost Children of Nananagua did not look lost any more. Their hangdog air was gone. Instead they looked tough and fit. Their faces were brown, their eyes glittered, they did not smell much, and they sang nearly in tune. In fact they seemed ready for anything.

'Congratulations,' said Daisy, curtsying slightly to El Gusano.

'We have found our courage,' said El Gusano with his rather too flashing smile. 'Though of course we are already brave. And now you are here, we will attack.'

'Attack?'

'We will rise up and set our mothers and fathers free from the Prison of the Parents,' said El Gusano.

'Really?' said Daisy. 'And when will this be?'

'Today!' cried El Gusano, with eyes like search-lights. 'Yeehah!'

'Er . . .' said Daisy. 'Is this –'

'We are the Lost Children of Nananagua. Who can resist us?'

From under the brim of her bowler, Daisy eyed the Lost Children and thought they looked pretty easy to resist. She glanced at Primrose, who was glancing at her. Then she exchanged glances with

Cassian and Pete. Most of the glances were accompanied by little shakes of the head. Everyone knew what they meant.

The Lost Children had no chance.

'It'll be a disaster,' murmured Daisy.

'You tell 'em, then,' murmured Pete.

'No, you,' murmured Primrose.

'I will if no one else will,' said Cassian, not bothering about murmuring, which he regarded as a sign of bendiness of mind. He jumped on to a barrel. 'Listen!' he cried. 'Frontal attack is not the way! Your only hope lies in stealth and guile!'

But everyone was too busy singing a feeble war song to listen.

The song ended.

'Stop!' cried Cassian.

'Let's GOOOOO!' cried El Gusano. 'Follow MEE to VICTOREE!'

Away they poured, making a noise like a flock of sheep that is thinking of giving up being vegetarian. Last to vanish over the hill was a figure who looked less bronzed and less fit. He had a sulky air, bulged slightly and was talking into a mobile phone. It was El Cook.

'Not a reliable person,' said Cassian.

Daisy sighed. Things were suddenly not going very well, and there was nothing she could do about it. 'Come,' she said, with grimmish resignation. 'Let us scale yonder mountain and watch.'

And up the mountain they stumped.

As the Darlings and their little charges climbed, the world spread out below them like a map. Far away was the sea, with the little white *Kleptomanic* gleaming in the bay. On the coast was Ciudad Olvidada. In the valley to the left, a cloud of vultures marked the Arbol del Muerto. In the valley to the right . . .

'Oops,' said Pete.

In the valley to the right was a square of barbed wire. Inside the square were many huts. At the corners of the square were towers that looked as if they were meant to contain guards. In the middle of one side of the square was a complicated building that looked like a heavily fortified gate.

And towards the gate was running a little crowd of something that looked like ants.

'Eek,' said Primrose, embarrassed.

For as you and I know, reader, these were not ants. They were the Lost Children of Nananagua.

Above the hot sigh of the breeze in the mountain grasses came a thin piping sound.

'Oh dear,' said Daisy.

The thin piping was war cries. The Lost Children of Nananagua were attacking the heavily fortified prison where their parents were being kept. For weapons they had bad spears, toy bows and hollow clubs made of lightweight plastic.

'Can't watch,' said Cassian.

But they did watch. And as they watched, their jaws dropped, one by one.

The Lost Children scampered up to the gate. They should have piled up against the barbed wire, giving themselves nasty scratches and tearing their clothes.

This is not what happened.

What happened was that the gates opened and the Lost Children scampered through. And when the last one was through, the gates closed again.

And that was that.

'Got them,' said Pete gloomily. 'Every man jack.'

'Child jack,' said Daisy. 'As if they knew they were coming.' But she spoke absently, for she was watching the events in the camp.

The Lost Children were being rounded up by

guards under the command of a couple of Nanas. From the huts had come rather bigger people. Their parents, perhaps. Everyone was hugging everyone else, in a welcome-to-prison-darling way.

But one child stood apart: a bulging child, wearing a bean-stained apron.

'El Cook,' said Daisy.

Two guards walked up to the bulging child and shook him warmly by the hand. Then they led him into a long hut with a chimney.

'He's dobbed them in,' said Pete. ''Orrible.'

The hut door closed.

'Treacherous devil,' said Cassian.

'And a lousy cook,' said Primrose. There was no bigger insult in her world.

'Hmm,' said Daisy, one nicely varnished nail tapping one well-kept tooth. As always, she was thinking.

El Cook was indeed a horrid traitor. But a person who could lead his friends into a prison could one day lead his enemies there too.

Whether he liked it or not.

'And over there,' said Cassian, pointing, 'is Vallenana, the Valley of Los Bungalos Guarding the Beige Door.'

The little party moved to the ridge. There indeed, far below, was the nice green valley. And there were the bungalows with their little groups of Nanas on their verandas.

And there in the ravine at the head of the valley was the rock wall with the shiny beige door.

Through the air from Vallenana there came the chink of hundreds of teacups being replaced on hundreds of saucers. The Nanas rose to their feet. The Beige Door opened. Someone came out and unrolled a scroll. There was the sound of a voice reading. It was far away, but some of the words floated up through the still evening air. 'Mumble, mumble, GREAT ONE pleased to announce that Nananagua is to have a king!'

'King?' said Daisy and Primrose.

'Ssh,' said Cassian.

'Coronation mumble mumble next week mumble,' said the voice. 'Mumble decree celebration rally in the National Stadium. The Junta will become dukes and will give good advice to the mumble mumble king. And La Nana, our beloved Great One, will be going on a cruise in her lovely new yacht, resting from her busy ruler's life and fulfilling a lifetime's ambition!'

More mumbling. The Nanas cheered. The

messenger, a Nana who could now be seen to be wearing black leather from head to toe, leaped on a motorbike and roared off, presumably bearing the glad tidings to the people of Ciudad Olvidada.

'Coronation?' said Primrose.

'New yacht?' said Cassian.

'You know what this means?' said Daisy.

'Wha?' said Pete.

'It means that Nanny Destiny is going to make the Chief King and steal the *Kleptomaniac*.'

'Yeah,' said Kazza gloomily. 'And celebration rally means they'll make us do displays.'

'Marching,' said Stalin.

'Mild singing,' said Horko, Yorko and Beans. 'Just you wait.'

'Lovely,' said Pete. 'Dead romantic, like.'

'That means we'll be stuck here forever, mutton-head,' said Primrose, her emotions getting the better of her.

'Manners!' said Cassian sternly. 'So. I'll look after things up here. First, I need to talk to the Chief.'

'Obviously. And we need to get down to the city and start a revolution,' said Daisy.

'Obviously,' said Cassian.

*

Cassian waved his sisters out of sight. Then he studied the wall above the Beige Door, using a powerful telescope. He saw a window from which glared a huge, familiar face with whirling eyes. He watched the curtains drawn over the window; the Chief was having an afternoon nap.

Cassian went to the Children's Camp to pick up the rope from the belfry. Then he crept over the mountain to Vallenana, and as dusk was falling made his perilous way to the top of the Cliff of the Beige Door. Here he waited until he heard the crash and howl of the Chief's bedtime. Then he attached the rope to the trunk of a stunted thorn and lowered himself down the cliff-face.

The Chief slept. It should have been so lovely, so cosy with the Royal Edward in the nice pink-and-gold room.

But the Chief was not happy. Ohnononono-nononononononononono. Not.

Something was missing. Promises had not been kept. Someone was saying one thing and meaning another.

The Chief writhed, tortured by uneasy dreams.

A great bird had landed on his shoulder. It was gripping him with its talons.

The Chief opened his eyes.

It was not a bird. It was Cassian.

The Chief opened his mouth to roar.

'Sshhh,' said Cassian. 'We are going to the volcano.'

The Chief closed his mouth.

Cassian was a little breathless. It had been a hard climb down the cliff to the window, and a difficult business picking the lock, even for him. But not nearly as difficult as what was to come. 'Up,' said Cassian. 'Quick. Now.'

The Chief said, 'Turn ze back.'

Cassian turned his back. All was quiet in the House of the Beige Door, except for dressing noises.

The dressing noises stopped. 'End if She finds out?' said the Chief.

'Her?' said Cassian. 'She smells of wee.' Childish and disgusting, of course, but so was the Chief.

'Hee hee hee,' said a little high royal-type voice. 'Und bum also.' Pause for high-pitched giggles and rolling-round-on-the-floor noises. Then the dressing noises resumed.

Cassian breathed a sigh of relief.

Out of the window they squeezed. Up the rope they swarmed. Up a long and gradually steepening slope they trudged under the light of a huge yellow moon.

'Where are we?' said the Chief. They had walked about 15 kilometres. He had stopped giggling after about five.

'On the slopes of El Volcano Grande.'

'Huh,' said the Chief. 'Ground not shaking. Not hot, und vere is flow of lava plus signs of pyroclastisches events?'

'Dunno,' said Cassian, who had some ideas of his own about these matters. 'On we go.'

On they went. The grass ran out. They were walking on rocks and grit. The moon was nearly as bright as day. Mist swirled around them.

'Thin clouds,' said the Chief, sounding more hopeful. 'Maybe is vast ective cone high above us, veiled from view but eruptink splendidly into dark-blue sky with stars gemixed. Oo I can hardly vait, come to me, mein lovely crater —'

'Ahem,' said Cassian.

There was no more uphill. They were standing in a place where the world went suddenly downhill. A sharp, stony ridge curved away to left and right, glowing faintly under the moon. The stone had a melted look, as if a long time ago it might have been liquid.

A very long time ago.

The Chief picked up a medium-sized boulder. He rolled it down the steep slope in front of him.

It bounded out of sight into the mist. They heard it go crash, crash, crash, crash, crash.

Then, faint but definite, splosh.

'Tchah,' said the Chief. 'Is a wolkano, OK. But not ective. Dormant. Even extinct, maybe.' His voice died to a cross mutter.

Cassian guessed he was talking to his bear. 'Well, seems like Nanny, er, Destiny made a mistake,' he said.

'Mistake?' said the Chief, spinning on his heel and beginning to march down the slope. 'LIES! She LIED!'

'Surely not,' said Cassian, with a sort of quiet satisfaction that he realized his sister Daisy must feel practically all the time. 'What an awful thing. Erm.' He was about to try something extremely bendy. 'Obviously you are . . . great friends with this Great One. Even if she tells you lies, I mean.'

'Oh ja,' said the Chief. 'She vas my Nana ven I

lived still as a tiny geezer in Kodsfjord, Royal Palace of Iceland, heppy heppy days.'

'Gg,' said Cassian, stunned.

'Und there vas a revolution und they out me throwed, bed, bed peoples, und ve vere torn asunder. I vent to engineering school. Und she worked as a bucko nanny on a royal yacht of my cousin Minimus of La Bamba. But she vas extra bossy and he was gettink sick of her, so he put her ashore here und ran away in his ship. Und she vorked for the then presidente, took over the country, trained the Nanas and vaited for a suitable schip to come along. She is vun powerful voman. Alvays,' said the Chief, 'she is vishink to run avay to sea.'

'Very laudable,' said Cassian, to hide his astonishment. 'But . . . of all the seaports in all the world, you had to bring the *Kleptomanic* into this one? Quite a fluke.'

'Is not fluke,' said the Chief. 'We are bonded, like small kink und Nana is bonded. She Calls me. Und now I vill be kink, und she vill go to sea in the *Kleptomanic*. Ven I give her the key to the ship.'

'Rr,' said Cassian. All this was bendy beyond his maddest imaginings. 'So. Well, congrats and all that. I mean nice to be king.'

'Ja,' said the Chief. His eyes were beginning to whirl, and his voice was a barmy mutter. 'Kink I vill be. Do zis! Do zat! Off mit his head!'

'But she tells you fibs,' said Cassian, wondering how to stop this maniac giving the *Kleptomanic* to his ex-nanny. 'I mean. If she'll lie about a volcano, where will it stop? Why don't you just forget it all. Come back to the ship, and bring the key obviously –'

'Key?' said the Chief. 'KEY? Everyone vanting the key. She vants it. You vants it. But I GOT IT. And of course I understand that you have brought me to false wolkano to make me giff you key. Hah! Out! Hence! Begone!'

All this time they had been walking swiftly downhill. At this point, they popped out of the mist. Mountains, valleys and sea lay spread in the greyish-yellow moonlight.

'Now I shall return to mein VORK,' cried the Chief. 'Das YIGSAW! UND I SHALL BE KINK!'

Cassian felt a deep and awful gloom, plus his feet hurt. As always, it was no use arguing with this loony. 'OK,' he said wearily. 'But while you sit behind that Beige Door waiting for this horrid person to make you kink, you think about who found your bear for you and got you a lovely new ship and has been kind and nice to you all this time. You silly, silly Chief,' said Cassian, frankly losing his rag.

'Impertinence!' cried the Chief. 'You vill call me Your Majesty plus shut up!' He stumped off towards Vallenana.

And Cassian knew that he had been undone by the bendiness of the Chief's mind. Now they would never get the key to the ship. They were here forever, while the Great One went on her cruise, and mad King Beowulf would rule with his new dukes. Nobody knows the trouble I see, thought Cassian.

Ramming his hands deep in his pockets, he began to trudge towards the road to the coast.

12

Late that night, the Darlings held a strategy meeting on the bridge of the *Kleptomanic II*. 'Celebrations in the National Stadium?' said the Captain. 'Will this not be boring?'

'Yes,' said Daisy. 'I hear they are going to want displays from the children of the Junta. To make their parents proud of them and impress the people. It is a very useful idea. For us, that is.'

'Wha?'

'Think about it,' said Daisy. 'The Junta or future

dukes or whatever they are now want their children to do them credit. El Generalissimo will want his children to look tough. The Dollars will want their children to look mild and clever. And El Simpatico and Derek will want little Kazza to look careful. What if they do not succeed, and the audience realizes these people are a hollow sham?'

'Then Nanny Disgusting will need other dukes.'

'Quite.'

'And she may find it hard to get some; so there will be a mad king with a Great One preparing to leave the country and no dukes to help him.'

There was a pause, during which everyone thought along the same lines.

'Which means,' said the Captain, 'that the people will be fed up, and Las Nanas will be without a leader, and there will be a revolution. Revolutions do not like kings. So we will get the Chief back, and the key and all that.' Her elegant fingers strayed towards the cocktail shaker. 'I am sure you have got a lovely plan already. But is there anything one could do to help?'

'You could play the joanna,' said Pete, blushing brick red. 'At the rally, like.'

The Captain's eyes settled on him, deep and dark.

'Brilliant,' she said. 'Do you know, I think I will.'

'I'll be there,' said Pete, blushing even brickier red. 'Inna front row.'

'Dear Pete.'

'Oh for goodness' sake,' said Daisy. 'Might I remind you we have work to do? Hats on, everyone. We've got a revolution to start.'

Off went the steam launch. Out got the Darlings and Pete. Uptown they trotted, and were merrily greeted by their little charges. That afternoon, they went for a Nice Walk. There were coronation posters everywhere, and whole families in the streets, looking nervous.

'What,' said Daisy to a passing normal hard-working Nananaguan family, 'is the problem?'

'Maybe this will be a bad thing, and the Junta will go power mad once they are dukes,' said the father, fiddling with his moustache.

'How I wish El Presidente Real Banana would come back,' said the mother, fiddling with hers.

'Relax and prepare for the revolution,' said Daisy.

'Anything you say, Nana,' said the father. And off he scuttled with his brood, to spread the word.

*

During the days that followed, advertisements for the rally in the National Stadium poured from the TV screens and radio speakers of the nation. The sergeant major spent hours drilling little Napoleon and Stalin, much to their disgust. A singing teacher came and trained the Dollar children in a mild song called 'Money is the Loveliest Thing', much to their embarrassment. And Strom Niggle the famous Hygiene Tutor came and instructed little Kazza in the Science of Careful Living, about which (much to her boredom) she was to give a speech.

As you may by now be suspecting, that was not exactly how it turned out.

Display Day dawned hot and smelly, and carried on like that. The National Stadium was in readiness.

Naturally it was the duty of Daisy, Primrose and Pete, as the nannies of the Junta, to take their little charges along to the stadium. They went through the stage door and on to the enormous stage and sat tidily, brogues together, hands in laps, casting discreet glances from under their bowler-hat brims at the crowd.

The stadium held 60,000 people. A brass band

was making grim oompah noises in the middle of the stage. After a while, the band stopped.

'Ladies and Gentlemen!' cried a great voice. 'We are proud to present to you our own Nananaguan hero, victor in the mountain wars, holder of the Order of the Bloodstained Condor . . . EL GENERALISSIMO!'

There was a tremendous crashing of boots. A squad of soldiers marched on to the stage and marched off again, leaving behind the figure of El Generalissimo. His moustache was waxed to points. His cap was hauled down over his eyes. His medals tinkled on his chest, and his breeches were enormous.

'Mphmahhh!' he snorted. People clapped and he saluted. Then something happened to his face.

'He's smiling,' said Daisy.

'Is that what it is?' said Primrose.

Napoleon and Stalin slipped their hands into Nanny Pete's.

'And now,' said El Generalissimo, 'I present to you, to show you how we are soldiers at home as well as in public, my sons!'

A storm of applause.

'Off you go, saucepans,' said Pete.

Off went Napoleon and Stalin, dressed in tiny uniforms with tiny model rifles.

The sergeant major had drilled them in the following routine: march across stage, march back, demonstrate unarmed combat, drink cup of fresh blood, salute, exit stage right to storms of applause.

The band struck up. The audience smiled. Its feet prepared to tap to a crisp military beat.

Its feet stopped in mid-air. What the band were playing was not marching music. It was dancing music, 'The Little Soldier Lads' by Floresque. Ballet-dancing music.

The two tiny soldiers rushed on to the stage with a hop and a hee. They leaped high in the air. Then they ran on their tippy-toes over to a big vase of lilies that stood by the side of the stage. Napoleon took both rifles. Stalin pulled two lilies from the vase and stuck one down the barrel of each gun. Then the two little fellows rushed into the middle of the stage, still on their tippy-toes, and bowed deeply to the crowd.

Looking down at the stalls, Daisy saw that the sea of faces had turned into a sea of open mouths. Someone at the back started clapping. The clapping died away. So the only people clapping were Daisy,

Primrose and Pete. They clapped loudly and loyally. The little soldiers looked breathless and happy. They climbed up into their chairs and sat down. Primrose dished out buttery biscuits. El Generalissimo seemed to have fainted. Silence filled the stadium, thick as cold porridge.

And to the front of the stage walked Minister and Madame Dollar.

'Time to get ready,' said Daisy. 'I'll tell you when.'

Away into the shadows offstage went Horko, Yorko and Beans, accompanied by Lost Horse Harry, a specialist horse rustler from the *Kleptomanic*.

Minister Dollar pulled out a wad of speech notes. He was looking extremely happy. If you are a future duke, it is always nice to watch one of your fellow future dukes get a large helping of sand on his salad. 'Ladies and gentlemen,' he said. 'I am happy to introduce our dear children, er, who will entertain you with a display of mild singing.'

On her chair, Daisy Darling spoke quietly into a portable radio. Somewhere in the backstage area a sliding door creaked open.

There was a thunder of hoofs, a creak of wagon wheels and a howl of cowboy yells. Horko, Yorko and Beans Dollar, mounted on pinto mustangs, thundered on to the stage. Behind them, Lost Horse Harry rode the buckboard of a mule wagon (whatever that means).

'Shoein' yer horse!' cried Horko as he thundered past the microphone.

'Western-style!' cried Yorko, sweeping off his hat.

'In one minute, painlessly!' cried Beans, sitting her rearing pinto like a pro.

Out came the forge and anvil from the wagon. Off leaped the Dollar children. Beans held the horse, Horko fitted the shoe and Yorko rasped the hoof, while Lost Horse Harry provided a running commentary, from time to time spitting terbacker juice into the front row of the stalls. 'Fifty-eight seconds, job done!' cried Lost Horse Harry.

'Yeehaaah!' cried the Dollar children, thundering offstage with the wagon bringing up the rear.

Daisy watched their parents totter feebly back to their chairs at the side of the stage. Derek had his hands to his mouth, and his eyes were large and horrified. El Simpatico strode up to the microphone with his eyes on full twinkle. He had every reason to be cheerful. If you are a minister, it is always nice to watch one of your fellow ministers get a handful of gravel in his ice cream.

'Good day to one and all,' said El Simpatico into the microphone. He looked slim, kindly, full of leadership. He opened his speech notes, which read as follows (the words in brackets, dear reader, remaining unsaid): 'And a safe, safe day to one and all. Remember, everyone. It is I (pause) and of course the rest of the Junta (curse them) who take the risks in life (but not many, thanks to Nanny Destiny, the Nanas and the police). So that you can live in perfect safety (like sheep, you fools). We will take the decisions (shiny smile). You can reap the benefits. (And so can we, since you have no idea what is really happening.) And we are sure of your support (because if we do not get it, you will all be in the Caboose, and the thumbscrews are greased and ready). Thank you. (Raise hands against storm of cheering. How can people be this stupid and live?) I wish you a safe and healthy coronation. Long live the King. And now, our dear adopted daughter Casuarinita, who used to be poor but now has a safe, safe family life, will give you an exhibition of Safe Behaviour.'

TWINGGG, said something high above the stadium.

A spotlight beam whizzed out of the lighting gallery.

Across the stadium stretched a line of light, fine as spider silk: a high wire.

'Goodness,' said Daisy.

'That girl,' said Primrose, 'is the bee's knees. Also the cat's pyjamas.'

'Ooh!' said the crowd.

For on to that spider-thin wire had bounced a tiny figure in a sequinned leotard. A tiny figure who was Kazza.

'Ah!' said the crowd.

For the figure in the leotard had started bouncing on the high wire. Up she soared, high above the uplifted faces in the stadium. Down she came, on to the wire. *Twingg*, went the wire. Up she went again, her sequins glittering as she somersaulted. Down she came, her feet looking for the wire –

Her feet missed the wire –

'Ng!' said the crowd.

As she plummeted, her smile did not falter. Her hooked fingers caught the wire. Once, twice she twizzled, and flung herself upward, sparkling. Down she came –

'Thooop!' said the crowd, drawing in breath.

– landed both feet on the wire, and skipped away into the darkness.

There was total silence.

Then there was a crash. That was Derek, fainting.

Then there was an explosion. That was El Simpatico, losing it. 'How DARE you!' he shrieked. 'You naughty, naughty, NAUGHTY girl! NEVER IN MY LIFE have I seen such an awful ghastly show-offy UNSAFE display of –'

But there were now other noises. There was a roar from the audience, who were looking up at the platform at the end of the wire, where Kazza was bowing elegantly, scattering a glittering cloud of sequins into the spotlight beam.

'– and WHO DO YOU THINK IS GOING TO PICK THOSE UP?' squealed El Simpatico, furious that people were looking at anyone but him.

Kazza gave one last bow and vanished into the scenery. 'AND GO STRAIGHT TO BED!' howled El Simpatico. He pasted on his smile. 'Ladies and gentlemen –'

'Boo,' said someone in the front row.

'Boo,' said two people in the second row.

'Boo,' said four people in the first, second and fifth rows. They were booing El Simpatico, not Kazza.

Reader, when booing spreads like this, it is not

long before the air is going to be full of vegetables.

Daisy rose. 'Come, everyone,' she said. 'We have made our point.'

The nannies of the Junta left the stadium, picking up their little charges as they went, and set off for a delicious tea on the *Kleptomanic*. Even the Captain's soulful piano playing could not drown the noise of breaking glass as the people of Ciudad Olvidada went to work on the official residences of the new dukes.

'The Great One is not going to be pleased,' said Daisy. 'Her dukes are a laughing stock. Her king is mad. Her power is waning.'

'But she is still guarded by Las Nanas,' said Pete.

'And she still wants the *Kleptomanic*,' said Cassian.

'Time for Phase Two,' said Daisy.

The Captain played a crippling arpeggio. 'The sort of Phase Two where you get into Vallenana by stealth and kidnap the Chief's teddy bear and make him give up this silly kink business and come back to the ship and release the children and their parents from the camp and leave this silly old Nana to stew in her own juice?'

'Goodness!' said Daisy. 'How did you guess?'

'A mother knows,' said Primrose, who was getting impatient. 'OK. Let's have the details.'

Daisy gave her companions the details, of which there were a lot. Next everybody went and packed a ditty bag with specialist equipment. Then they went ashore and headed for the mountains.

All was quiet in the prison camp, where the Lost Children of Nananagua were held captive with their parents.

A waning moon peered from an inky sky. In the huts, everyone was asleep. But who is this figure creeping across the compound?

Wait for it.

Like all cooks, even lousy ones, El Cook was good at doing two things at the same time. Tonight, he was combining dreaming with snoring. In his dream, people were bringing him huge mounds of white ice cream topped with blackish chocolate sauce. Every time they brought a new mound, men in tabards blew trumpets. Yummsnore, went El Cook. Yummsnore.

'Stone me, what a racket,' said a voice somewhere.

El Cook turned over. The next pile of ice cream was green. When he stuck his spoon into it, it put out two green hands and grabbed him. He opened his mouth to yell, but the ice cream put a third hand into his mouth, and when he tried to bite the hand he found that it was made of cloth, and smelly cloth at that.

'Sssh,' said the ice cream in his ear.

El Cook opened his eyes. He shut them again, quickly. Not quickly enough, though.

''Ello, podgy,' said a voice. This time it did not belong to the ice cream. It belonged to a person with an unshaven chin, a black mask round his eyes and a jersey that in the light seeping through the window El Cook could see was stripy.

'Do not think of screaming, "Help, Nanas",' said the voice. 'It will do no good, because the Nanas are the other side of the camp and besides you may have a nasty accident.'

'Accident?' said El Cook, round the hanky stuffed in his mouth. 'Why?'

'Because I will give you one,' said the burglar, his grin dreadful in the dim light. 'Now, hup you get and orf we go.'

El Cook shoved his shaking feet into their sneakers.

'Out the door, turn right,' said the burglar. 'And remember.'

'Remember what?'

'About accidents.'

'Ooer,' said El Cook, whose mind had shrunk to a pinpoint of raw terror, and who could not of course see that the burglar's fingers were crossed behind his stripy back, the burglar being Pete Fryer, the diamondest geezer who ever swiped spoon.

They went out of the door and turned right. Someone had cut a hole in the barbed-wire fence. 'Go through,' said the burglar.

El Cook went through.

'Stop wibbling,' said the burglar.

El Cook could not stop wibbling.

'All right, wibble faster,' said the burglar.

El Cook wibbled faster. He wibbled out into the darkness beyond the lights and (with the burglar behind him) up a steep hillside studded with cactus and boulders. Probably there were snakes. Up some mountain they went. Up some more mountain they went. El Cook was running sweat, very thirsty and fearsomely hungry. Just when he thought he was going to die of hunger, thirst, terror and sore feet, the mountainside seemed to open up in front of him and light dazzled his eyes.

An arm bearing a cake came out of the dazzle. El Cook ate it; the cake, that is. His eyes cleared.

He saw a small stone room, with bunks up one wall. On the bunks, six children were sleeping nicely. At a table in the middle were two nannies and an oily-faced boy –

Suddenly he knew where he was. He was back in the Camp of the Lost Children, where they had lived before their capture. And the two girls at the table were . . . the small, eager nannies of the sleeping children, who were the children of the Junta. And the oily-faced boy –

El Cook even remembered his name. 'Cassian!' he said.

'That's me,' said Cassian. 'Welcome to our little cave in the hills.'

'You would like to sit down,' said the smaller and pinker of the two nannies. 'And then we will explain how you are going to help us break into Nanny Destiny's beige sitting room.'

'No,' said El Cook. But he sat down anyway, because his knees seemed suddenly not to be working any more.

Daisy explained.

El Cook said, 'No way.'

'Way,' said Primrose. 'Or Pete will set fire to your trousers. Won't you, Pete?'

Kindly Pete had gone pale at the very idea. 'Grr,' he managed to say. He fixed a snarl to his rugged yet civil features, and turned them on El Cook. 'You do what you're told, sonny. Otherwise it's, Oo me bum's burning and no fire brigade in sight. Geddit?'

'Yeah,' said El Cook, in a very small voice.

'Good,' said Daisy. 'Well. Bedtime. Then up we pack and off we go.'

That night El Cook was closely guarded, for fear of treachery. Next morning off they went, down the mountain and into the valley. The bottom of the valley was green and flat. Stout cows grazed, and little clumps of trees scented the air with their flowers. And on the far horizon was a line, drawn as if with a sharp pencil across the green.

'What's that?' said Daisy, feeling a certain chill.

'The Vallenana fence,' said Cassian. 'As described by Luggage, remember? Razor wire, minefields, all that? Protecting the bungalows of Las Nanas. Which in turn protect the Beige Door.'

'Ooer,' said El Cook, wibbling like a blancmange.

'Less of that,' said Daisy. 'All a fence like this means is that someone has got something to hide. Eh, children?'

The tinies of the Junta raised their little hands in the air and gave three cheers, they knew not why.

'Jolly good,' said Daisy. 'Now then. Remember the plan we made. Pete, get the fetters out of the ditty bag and chain us together.'

More cheers.

'And remember, Cook,' said Primrose. 'Trousers.'

'Oh, er, grr,' said Pete, locking fetters on the ankles of all and sundry.

'Ready?' said Daisy. 'Off we go!'

13

The security guard in front of the gate in the Vallenana fence was called Brutus Strength. He was eating a sausage sandwich and feeling suspicious. Both these things were normal and part of the security guard's job. The other part was being completely useless. Brutus Strength was good at that too.

So when he saw the procession coming down the road towards him, he took another bite of his sandwich and did a bit of thinking, or what passed for thinking with him.

It was an odd procession. There was a bulging boy in front. Behind were nine people, shortest first, tallest last. The people were all chained together. They were singing:

> *O what a lovely day to be*
> *MARching into captivitee.*

They clanked up to the gate and stopped.

'Yeah?' said Brutus.

There was a silence. Someone in the group hissed, 'Trousers!' The bulging boy jumped as if he had been stung by a wasp. 'I have here some prisoners for, er, She Who Cannot Be Named,' gabbled the bulging boy, all on one note.

'Who?'

'She Who Cannot Be Named.'

'Yeah,' said Brutus. 'But what's she called?'

'She Who –'

'Lissen,' said the person at the back, who needed a shave and was in fact Pete Fryer. 'She is called La Nana, alias Nanny Destiny, alias the Great One, am I right? And El Cook here is one of her number-one spies. Bringing in some slaves, like he mentioned.'

Brutus Strength frowned. His mind worked better

when he was frowning, not that that meant much. He seemed to recognize the bulging person. 'Oh,' he said. 'Right. Yeah. Course. El Cleaner, yeah?'

'Cook,' said El Cook.

'Same thing,' said Brutus Strength.

'It is not the same thing,' said a smallish slave with pale-blue eyes and yellow hair.

Brutus looked at her, then decided it was safer not to. He said, 'File on, file.'

The file filed on. As the little blonde slave went past, she said to Brutus, 'Little sauce on your sandwich?'

'Gimme,' said Brutus.

The little slave handed him a bottle of goo from her backpack. Brutus squeezed on four greedy dollops and threw the bottle away.

'Happy trails,' said the little slave, smiling rather worryingly. The file marched on.

'Where now?' hissed El Cook.

'Straight ahead,' said Daisy.

Straight ahead were neat Nana bungalows from which came the clink of teacups, the riffle of playing cards and the sharp shrieks of Nanas whose muscles had been sprained in arm-wrestling bouts. Straight behind, someone was screaming.

'What's that noise?' said Cassian.

'I think it's the security guard,' said Primrose. 'I think he ate my sauce.'

There was a roar as of jet engines and the howl of a slipstream. Brutus shot past, flame pouring from his trouser legs. He rocketed to a colossal height, looped the loop and flew at high speed into a distant crag. The crag collapsed. Brutus zoomed on.

'What sort of sauce was that?' said Daisy.

'Hot sauce,' said Primrose. 'Guaranteed to put zing in your zandwich.'

'How true,' said Daisy, eyeing the distant plume of dust that was all that remained of the crag.

'I'se bein' good,' whimpered El Cook. 'I'se bein' good.'

'Of course you are,' said Daisy, and pointed out an attractive bird to distract her charges from half a dozen granite-faced Nanas who were staring at them.

'An' just up ahead,' said El Cook, 'you will see the Beige Door. Ooer.'

'You are right to be nervous,' said Daisy. 'It seems rather well guarded.'

And indeed, on either side of the door there stood a vast grim Nana.

'What we need,' said Cassian, 'is that guard back.'

'Guard!' shouted little Napoleon, who was having the time of his life.

'Fishface!' shouted little Stalin, who was also having the time of his.

High above, the dot that was Brutus Strength seemed to pause. Then it grew small – not because it was going away, but because the chain gang in front of the Beige Door were seeing it head-on. High in the air, a voice without brains cried, 'YOU'RE NICKED!' And down came Brutus Strength, hands clawed in the nicking position, hurtling towards the chain gang from behind.

'Duck!' yelled Daisy.

For a moment, Brutus was heading straight for them. He howled down the ravine and through the group, making a grab at Primrose, whom he rightly blamed for his present difficulties. Primrose stepped nimbly aside.

'AIEEEEE!' cried Brutus Strength, trying to put on the brakes, then remembering that he did not have any.

There was a splintering crash. The guard Nanas lay scorched, one either side of the Beige Door, planets spinning around their heads. Confused noises and clouds of smoke issued from the end of the ravine.

Where the Beige Door hung open from a single hinge.

'It is time to introduce ourselves to Nanny Disaster!' cried Daisy.

'Destiny,' said Cassian.

'Whatever. Pass the key. Unlock chains and forward!'

Pete passed the key. They unlocked the chains. Forward they went.

There was a front hall, nicely decorated with pictures of royal tinies and a grandmother clock and a beige carpet thickly strewn with door splinters. Off the front hall was a well-equipped day nursery, in which the Darlings left the children of the Junta to do their worst with the crayons provided. There was an inner door with a Brutus Strength-shaped hole in it. Beyond the inner door was a charming parlour with beige chintz armchairs. On the walls were signed pictures of mad kings and queens. On the parlour table was a tray of tea and biscuits. In the middle of the tray of tea and biscuits, disturbing its tidy look, was

Brutus Strength, still smoking faintly from the trouser legs.

'Well?' said Primrose.

'Nobody here,' said Daisy. 'This must be the sitting room.'

'I don't like it,' said Pete.

'Nor do –'

Click, went a switch. The corner of the room was suddenly flooded in an unearthly beige glare. And there, bolt upright in a chair, knees together, teacup in hand, little finger crooked, sat a nanny.

She was a small nanny, with a smooth pink face and mild blue eyes. It was the smooth pink face whose portrait hung on walls all over Nananagua. Daisy studied her with interest. A nanny who had been sitting in a beige room into which a security guard had been fired though two locked doors might be expected to be rather shaken. Not this nanny. Daisy cast an experienced eye at her saucer. Not a drop spilt. This was a nanny with nerves of steel, or possibly no nerves at all.

'Hello,' said Primrose to the nanny. 'You must be Nanny Dysentery.'

'Destiny.'

'Whatever.'

The nanny took a sip of tea. 'Oo,' she said. 'Uzzums wuzzums ickle.'

Daisy repressed an urge to sneer. This was the kind of nanny little Darlings ate for breakfast. She opened her mouth to ask the nanny if she had seen the Chief Engineer. But the words seemed somehow to stick halfway up her throat. Odd.

'Yes, liddle one?' said the nanny. 'What does the liddle one wish to say to Nana?'

Daisy found her head was swimming.

The nanny's eyes did not move. 'You wanted to ask Nana somefing, duckie?'

'Where,' said Daisy, 'is . . .?' No good. The awful china-blue eyes were sucking her will. She was a tiny little girl again. Her only ambition was to go into a nursery and Play Nicely not getting her Pinny Filfy until Teatime, when she would have stale cake and Eat It All Up.

Cassian said, 'We want the Chief.' Something seemed amiss with his sister. Belt slipping, cog failing to engage, something like that.

The blue eyes turned on him. 'Nana finks you are talking about His Royal Highness Chief Engineer Crown Prince Beowulf of Iceland (deposed), holder of the Order of the Codfish and Volcano, B.Eng.

(Reykjavik), future King of Nananagua.' The sandy brows came down a millimetre. 'A ROYAL PERSONAGE! Where are your MANNERS! IN THE CORNER! NOW, THIS MINUTE!'

The room spun before Cassian's eyes. His feet started moving, even though he told them not to. He found himself looking at two walls meeting at an angle. There was beige wallpaper with beige bunnies on. Someone, somewhere, was thinking: this horrible old woman has hacked Cassian Darling's mind. He recognized the thoughts as his own. But there was nothing he could do about them.

'Oi, Nanny,' said a voice. 'We want the Chief, and we want him now, so tell us where you're hiding him and things won't get nasty.' It was Primrose; a Primrose standing with her hands on her hips, deeply aware that she was all out of special foods, but not about to let that stop her.

'Nana always makes fings nice,' said the nanny, turning the eyes on her.

Primrose's own eyes were mild and blue, and now they narrowed a fraction. The room was darkening at the edges and her thoughts seemed to be wading through syrup. Thin syrup by adding lemon juice, said the cook in Primrose. Primrose managed a sour thought.

Suddenly she knew what to do. 'Nana,' she said.

'Ickle wickles,' said the nanny, disgustingly.

'Good dear lovely kind pretty nice Nana,' said Primrose, hoping that her brother and sister were far enough out in deep space not to be able to hear what was happening. She edged forward.

'Hold it right there!' cried the nanny in a voice like a whiplash.

'Lovely sweet good merciful angelic wise excellent Nana,' said Primrose, fixing her eyes half a metre to the right of Nanny Destiny's. She had seen mad people do this. Perhaps Nanny Destiny would think she was mad. Also, it meant that she did not have to look into those ghastly blue eyes that were trying to suck out her mind like a hedgehog sucks cow's milk (you will see, dear reader, even being in the same room as those eyes affected the brain).

'Ickle pree,' said Nanny Destiny. Then, sharply, 'Keep your distance!'

Too late. Primrose had gritted her teeth and covered the last two metres at a sort of run. Her sticky little right hand had grabbed Nanny Destiny's left. Her sticky little left hand had grabbed Nanny Destiny's teacup and tipped it into Nanny Destiny's lap.

'Yarrr!' cried Nanny Destiny, leaping to her feet and trying to dust hot tea out of her knickers. Primrose, swift as always, grabbed the teapot and started pouring Earl Grey into Nanny Destiny's brogues.

'Aiee!' howled La Nanny Destiny.

'Goodness!' cried Daisy, restored to her right mind.

'Nice one, Prim!' cried Cassian, unhacked.

'Curse your black hearts, ye sewer scum!' cried La Nana, hopping round the room on one foot.

'Cassian,' said Primrose. 'Door.'

Cassian looked round. He saw a door. He opened it. Nanny Destiny hurtled past him on one leg, clean out of control. 'Nooo!' she cried as she shot through. The sound was cut off short by the slam of the door.

There was the sort of silence that falls when two girl nannies and a boy engineer are catching their breath, a security guard is in a tea tray with slight concussion and his trousers on fire, and a burglar is out of the room –

Out of the room? Wha?

Sorry.

You will have noticed, reader, that Pete Fryer has played no part in the rather worrying events reported above.

This is because Pete Fryer had been casing the joint.

Behind its chintzy sitting room, the House of the Beige Door was hewn from the living rock, more like a mole rat's lair than a nanny's residence. There were staircases, bedrooms, larders, dungeons, nurseries and oubliettes –

Oubliettes?

Forget oubliettes for the moment. Let us concentrate on the nurseries.

Right.

Pete had gone out of a door. There was a Formica map on the wall. FIRE MAP, it said. BE AWARE OF YOUR NEAREST EXIT. OR FACE LEGAL PROBLEMS. MINIMUM PENALTY 2 YEARS PLUS REPTILES AND THUMBSCREWS. THIS IS YOUR DUTY AS A CITIZEN. Pete perused it briefly. Then he went up some stairs, along a corridor, and came finally, guided by his burglar's instincts, to a door with a gold coronet on it. Gently turning the handle, he pushed it open.

It was a pink room trimmed with gold. A soft light

came through pink muslin curtains and fell gently on an enormous cot. In the cot lay Chief Engineer Crown Prince Beowulf of Iceland, King-to-be of Nananagua, clutching the Royal Edward, his teddy bear. His spiked helmet was over one eye. His mouth was open and he was snoring horribly. Round his neck, on its short titanium chain, was the key to the *Kleptomanic*.

Pete's feet took over. He slid across the room, shoe-soles caressing the floor in a silent embrace. His hand went to the key, prepared to close on it. Blue sea, warm sun, no more disgusting Nananagua, said the metal.

'Mschmfrumm,' said the Chief.

'Chicken,' said Pete, jerking his hand away.

The Chief's eyes flicked open 'Vas?' he said.

'Chicken jalfrezi, take it easy,' said Pete.

'Ach,' said the Chief. His eyes bulged. 'AAAAAH!' he roared. He had learned through bitter experience that at moments of high tension someone usually stole the Royal Edward, and he was ready for them. He rolled on his face, masking the precious bear under many kilos of royal blubber.

''Scuse me,' said Pete, reaching again for the key chain round the Chief's neck. But the chain was short, and the Chief's head was big.

'AAAAH!' roared the Chief again. 'Leave me! I vill not GO!'

A confused burst of shouting came from downstairs. Pete found that he was sweating lightly. In all his burgling days he had never come across a state of affairs as moody as this one. 'Catch ya later,' he said, and went for the door.

In the sitting room, things were somewhat tense. The Darling children were standing round a small closed-circuit TV screen. It showed the scene in the ravine. Or as much of the scene as was visible through the forty or fifty very large Nanas who were standing looking threateningly at the wreckage of the Beige Door.

Pete put his thumb on the intercom button.

'One step closer, and the Great One gets it,' he barked into the microphone.

'I already told them that,' said Primrose.

'The Chief won't come,' said Pete. 'He thinks we want his bear.'

Daisy said, not without impatience, 'May I point out that we are in a hostage situation without a hostage and that this is not the time for going on and on about bears?'

'Sorry,' said Pete, crestfallen. 'So where is Nanny Dogbowl?'

'Destiny.'

'Whatever.'

'In there,' said Daisy, whose freckles were standing out against the unusual pallor of her skin.

Pete walked over to the door through which the Nana had disappeared.

'Careful,' said Primrose, in a distinctly shaky voice.

'She's got a screw loose,' said Cassian.

Pete had never heard them so alarmed. 'Relax,' he said, with a confidence he probably did not feel, though it was hard to tell, because tattoos tend to hide feelings. He rapped with his knuckles on the door. 'Oi in there,' he said.

'Lemme outies wouties,' said the voice of Nanny Destiny. An odd voice. Seeming to come not from *behind* the door, but *below* it.

'Ah,' said Pete, casting his mind back to the fire map. He sat down in a chair.

'Er,' said Daisy. 'Should we not, well, hurry up a bit?'

'Werl,' said Pete, 'we need a bit of a planning session.'

'Ah,' said Cassian, for whom plans were infinitely soothing.

'Shoot,' said Primrose.

The debate commenced. And while it is going on, reader, it is time that you got up to date with oubliettes, as promised.

An oubliette is a sort of dungeon. Its name comes from the French word for forgetting. If you have got an oubliette, you use it for people you never want to see again. Think of a deep hole, maybe with an underground river at the bottom of it, maybe with spikes, preferably with both, and certainly with crocodiles, or possibly alligators. Very nasty people usually have an oubliette opening off the sitting room. Nanny Destiny was exactly that nasty a person. And it was through the oubliette door that, maddened by hot tea in lap and shoes, she had accidentally run.

'So,' said Pete. 'That's the picture.'

'Time to make a deal,' said Primrose.

'Daisy can do the talking,' said Cassian.

'Willingly,' said Daisy, with a charming gesture of her arm.

Pete opened the oubliette door. Three Darling heads looked through.

Not through. Down.

'Helpies,' said a small voice.

As their eyes got used to the dark, the Darlings realized that they were looking down a circular shaft lined with stone. Five metres below, a bit of iron stuck out of the side of the shaft. Sitting on the bit of iron was Nanny Destiny. From below came the sound of running water and a sort of coughing grunt that Daisy recognized as the call of the hungry alligator, or possibly crocodile.

'Get me out of here,' said Nanny Destiny.

'Say please.'

There was an unpleasant grinding noise, as of teeth. 'Please.'

'On condition,' said Daisy.

'What condition?'

'That we can have the Chief back. And give orders for the release of the Lost Children and their parents.'

'Naughtiness!' hissed the Nana. 'Naughty bad wicked naughtiness! Go and stand in the –'

'Well, nice knowing you,' said Daisy, writing on a piece of paper. 'Give our best to the alligators. Or crocodiles.' She started to close the door.

'Wait!' cried Nanny Destiny, in a new, rather

anxious voice. 'If you're very, very good –'

'Byee!' cried everybody.

'Wait!' cried Nanny Destiny. 'What do you want me to do?'

'Tell the Chief to come with us.'

'No,' said Nanny Destiny.

'Down she goes,' said Pete.

'He doesn't want to go, does he?' said Nanny Destiny.

'Ner,' said Pete. 'Actually not.'

'But I am going to bring him down to Ciudad Olvidada for his coronation,' said Nanny Destiny. 'And you can ask him again there.'

'Yes,' said the Darlings. 'All right. But we want the Lost Children and the Lost Parents. I am sending down a Form of Safe Conduct.'

Even halfway down the shaft of the oubliette with her knickers soaked in tea, Nanny Destiny's will was horribly powerful. Feeling slightly dazed, Daisy put the paper she had been writing on into a little beige basket and lowered it into the oubliette. 'Sign here,' she said. 'Then we will haul you up on this rope made out of your curtains.'

'My lovely curtains!'

'Where does the mustard live?' said Cassian.

'Why?'

'Because I would like to throw some to the crocodiles – or are they alligators? – to make you taste better.'

There was a silence. Then Nanny Destiny said, in a weak, flat voice, 'Where do I sign?'

'At the bottom,' said Daisy. 'In ink.'

Five minutes later, Nanny Destiny was standing in the corner of her beige sitting room, staring at the wall so Pete and the Darlings would not see her terrible eyes.

She said, 'You will be sorry, you know.'

'Time will tell,' said Primrose.

Pete Fryer's battered but kindly features were decorated with a worried expression. 'She'll hypnotize everyone,' he hissed to Daisy.

'So she thinks,' said Daisy. 'But we know she's planning to steal the ship and run away. Wait till the people hear.'

'Have faith,' said Primrose.

'Silly old fool,' said Cassian.

'Yur,' said Pete. He tapped his teeth with the Form of Safe Conduct, and took a deep breath. 'Off we go, then. And may the best, er, person win.'

'Ssss,' said Nanny Destiny.

'And mind you bring our Chief.'

Nanny Destiny laughed. The beige wallpaper in front of her face began to smoulder and melt. 'My own little kingy wingy –'

'Crown Princy Wincy,' pointed out Daisy, passionate for accuracy.

'– wants to stay with his Nana. And if anyone says different, I say they are WRONG. You are all getting sleepy weepy. Very, very sleeepy weeepy . . .'

'LA LA LA,' cried Primrose, drowning her. 'She's trying to hypnotize us. Let's get out of here. Sing!'

They sang. They sang like dwarves going off to the mine, only louder and out of tune. They got the children of the Junta out of the day nursery and made them join in. The Nanas outside the ruins of the Beige Door parted when they saw the Form of Safe Conduct. The Darlings went on, still singing. They trotted out of the gate and up the mountainside, while behind them the village of bungalows swarmed like a well-poked ant's nest. Still singing, but seriously out of breath, they trotted down the valley.

'Right,' said Daisy. 'First, to the camp. We will show the Safe Conduct to the guards, so they will have to let out El Gusano and El Presidente Real Banana and everyone. Then off we go to Ciudad Olvidada and the coronation. Which I think may be rather interesting as coronations go.'

'Accidents will happen,' said Cassian.

'Heh heh,' said Primrose.

'Right!' cried Daisy. 'Off, off and away!'

Off, off and away they went.

14

It was Coronation Day.

Just after breakfast, shepherds tending sheep on the mountains above Vallenana heard the tolling of a great bell from inside the Cliff of the Beige Door. Soon after that, a chimney rising from the greensward among the bungalows began to belch enormous volumes of black smoke. Soon the grass and the bungalows had completely disappeared, and a dark carpet lay over the smiling green.

Under the smoke, machinery roared and clanked.

Open your eyes, your eyes.

The Chief opened them.

Your jigsaw is loaded. It is your Coronation Day. Off we goooooooo.

'ICH DO NICHT WANNA –'

It is tiiiiiime.

'NEIN.'

A confused punching and slapping.

'NEEEEEIIINNN! EDVARD! SCHE HAS STOLEN MEIN EDVAAAAAAARD!'

You are getting sleeeeeeepy. Falling under my speeeeell.

'NEIN I AM NOT. YOU HAF SCHTOLEN MEIN EDVARD. KOM TO PAPA, EDVARD!'

Now you are being a silly billy. No coronation, no Edward. Well?

'JA. I SUPPOSE.'

Wait a minute. Where is the keeeeeeeey? That was round your neckk.

'VOT KEY? I NEVER SEEN NO KEY.'

The ship keeeeeeeeeeeeeeeeeeeeeeeeeey.

'OH, THAT KEY. ALVAYS IS CAUSING TROUBLE. SO I FLUSCH HIM DOWN LAVATORY.'

234

Aaaaaaaaaaaaaagh. Naughty. Very, very naughty.
'SO VOT YOU GONNA DO ABOUT IT?'
Nothing now. After, though? Ssssssssssssssssssssssssss.

At eleven o'clock, there was a stirring in the smoke
flooring Vallenana. Shapes emerged, trailing
threads of oily black vapour. It was a convoy: three
black vans with blacked-out windows, then an
armoured car, then an armoured van with a gold
crown on top, then an articulated truck carrying
a shrouded burden. The convoy took off at top
speed down the mountain road towards Ciudad
Olvidada.

There were posters all over the city. BY ORDER, they
said.

NANNY DESTINY, OUR GREAT ONE, WILL THIS
DAY BE HANDING OVER POWER TO KING
BEOWULF I. CORONATION 12 NOON SHARP ON
THE CEREMONIAL PLATFORM IN FRONT OF
THE GREAT HALL OF THE PEOPLE. LOYAL
SUBJECTS WILL WATCH FROM THE PRINCIPAL
SQUARE. CHEERING COMPULSORY. THIS MEANS
YOU.

By half past eleven the Principal Square was
crowded with people. It was a glum, weary crowd,
except when the Nanas were looking, at which point
it gave a big false smile. Mostly it stood in gloomy
silence, waiting.

At a quarter to twelve, the hum became a buzz.
Then, with a full-throated roar, the convoy swept
into the square. It came in at high speed. The Nanas
saluted. The convoy roared up ramps on to the
platform and turned hard left.

'Wait for it,' said El Gusano, faking a yawn.

For some time, Cassian, El Gusano and the Lost
Children had been smearing oil and grease just
about where the convoy would turn hard left.

'Whee!' cried El Gusano, clapping his hands. 'I
am a GENIUS!'

The fierce black vans in front were suddenly
transformed into figure-skaters. They swooped
elegantly to and fro, out of control. They removed
eleven palm trees and piled up against the far wall
of the Great Hall of the People with a crash like

a bomb bursting. Smoke covered the scene. The crowd drew in its breath.

'I am so cool,' said El Gusano.

Any minute now the crowd would start laughing and the job would be done.

But the crowd did not start laughing. Instead, it let out its breath in a long, nervous whoosh.

Out of the smoke came two vehicles, still moving. One was the armoured van with the crown on the roof. The other was the articulated truck carrying the shrouded form of the giant machine. Both of them had big spikes on their tyres, for grip. The vehicles stopped, one on either side of the platform. Nanas started taking the big machine off the articulated lorry. Other Nanas started to set up a huge golden throne in the middle of the platform.

'Relax,' said Daisy. 'The woman is doomed.'

'Well doomed,' said Primrose.

'Ye-es,' said Cassian. But he did not like the look of the machine. He did not like the look of it at all.

The Darlings moved closer to the platform.

Primrose cocked an ear. 'What's that sound?' she said. From the direction of the van with the crown came the sound of sobbing, tiny and distant. 'There,' she said.

'Someone sobbin' in a van,' said El Gusano, who did not approve of weakness. 'Here she comes.'

'Block your ears,' said Daisy, handing out plugs.

Two giant Nanas took up positions one on either side of the platform. And into the centre walked with silly little steps the silly little figure of Nanny Destiny.

Up to the microphone she went. 'Ahem,' she said in her small, high voice. 'Funny old weather we are having for the time of year.'

A strange rustling swept through the Principal Square of Nananagua. It was the sound of tens of thousands of people saying very politely that it looked like it was coming on to rain.

'Naughty,' said La Nana, sweeping the crowd with her shallow blue eyes. 'Naughty, *naughty*!'

Daisy shivered. The temperature in the square had dropped by 20 degrees.

'You have been bad, all of you,' said La Nana. 'People have been trying to bully their Nana! Other Nanas would have made you all kneel on dried peas in the corner. But your Nanny Destiny is merciful. I do what I do because I have to do it, and it hurts me more than it hurts you.' She began to purr like a ghastly cat. 'And I have a plan for you, my children. A marvellous plan that you will lurrrve.'

The audience nodded eagerly, hypnotized.

'Why doesn't this affect us?' said Primrose.

'Because we have wax in our ears,' said Daisy, lip-reading.

'Wha?' said Cassian.

'Well,' said Nanny Destiny. 'Here is my plan. We have had enough of governments. We do not like Juntas. They are not worthy.'

'Not worthy,' murmured the crowd.

'I am leaving you for a lovely holiday on the sea,' said La Nana. 'At the end of my cruise I may come back. Meanwhile, my Nanas will look after you and keep you safe. The head of the country will be someone royal, because royals are so important. And I have found you a worthy king.'

'Worthy, worthy,' murmured the crowd.

'See what she's got under her arm?' said Daisy.

'Stone me,' said Pete, lip-reading.

'It's the Royal Edward,' said Primrose, lip-reading too.

'So where's the Chief?' said Cassian, lip-writing.

'A ruler of the blood royal,' said Nanny Destiny, rolling the words around her tongue. 'From a family bred to rule. Ladies and gentlemen, or should I say subjects, please welcome your new monarch!'

'JA!' said a voice. 'IS ME!' And from out of the armoured van with the crown on top there shambled an enormous figure in a military uniform and a spiked helmet, with the Order of the Codfish and Volcano glittering on the breast of his tunic and tears glittering on his flabby cheeks.

'People of Nananagua!' cried La Nana. 'Good people who promise never again to be naughty! I have the honour to present to you His Ever So Royal Gracious and Noble Highness King Beowulf I.'

'Oh,' said everyone in the audience. The weird figure of the new king seemed to be breaking Nanny Destiny's spell.

'The words you are groping for,' said Nanny Destiny in a low, dangerous voice, 'are, "All hail!"' She beckoned the Chief Engineer. 'Step forward, Your Royal Highness. Sit on the throne and Nanny Destiny will crown you!'

'Vere is MEIN EDVARD?' cried the Chief in a great voice.

'Later,' hissed La Nana. 'When you have done your dutykins for Nana.'

'I VANT HIM,' cried the Chief.

The crowd was stirring now. The spell was definitely lifting. The Darlings took the wax out of their ears.

'That's as may be,' said Nanny Destiny. 'Now then, everyone, simmer down.' The temperature was dropping again.

Suddenly, Pete was gone from Daisy's side. He sprinted up the steps and on to the platform, head down, running like a fly half. His hand went out and twitched the Royal Edward from under Nanny Destiny's arm. And Nanny Destiny yelled, 'Guards! Guards!' and about twenty Nanas poured out of the wings and pounced on Pete. But out of the heaving scrum of Nanas shot a small, dirty-brown creature. It soared through the air towards Cassian, who put out an arm, caught it and started to sprint towards the quay where the *Kleptomanic*'s launches were waiting, weaving between the legs of the big people in the crowd and shouting, 'Chief! I've got the Royal Edward! Come and get him!'

'EDVAAARD!' bellowed the Chief, and started lumbering towards Cassian.

'Stop!' cried Nanny Destiny.

The crowd were making lowing noises, like muddled cattle.

Cassian ran on. 'Catch!' he shouted, flung the Royal Edward towards the Chief and shinned up a lighting tower. From this vantage point he saw the Chief with his hands out, ready to catch the Royal Edward.

'Nice pass,' said Primrose to Daisy.

Reader, she spoke too soon.

From out of left field came a Nana like a streak of gingham lightning. She thundered across the Chief's bows, hurtled across the platform and walloped into a wall. Bricks fell. The Nana came to rest.

But as the Nana had passed the Chief, she had put out an enormous hand and grabbed the Royal Edward out of the air.

Daisy saw the Chief's face grow endlessly long, his mouth grow ludicrously round. The crowd was making an ugly roar now. It was deeply, deeply cross, because the spell had been broken by Disorder, and it now realized it had been messed about with.

'Get the bear!' yelled Cassian above the din.

The Nana lay under a small pile of bricks, her eyes crossed and the Royal Edward in the crook of her arm. The Chief lay on the stage, his heels drumming in a Force Nine tantrum.

'Leave it to mee!' cried El Gusano, and he shot away through the crowd towards the Nana with the bear.

'Leave it to mee!' cried Nosey Clanger, and shot away through the crowd towards the same Nana.

From his lighting tower, Cassian could see the whole thing unfold.

The streak that was Nosey zoomed through the crowd. So did the streak that was El Gusano. They collided at a speed of 50 kilometres an hour. There was a sound like two coconuts imitating a horse's hoof. Both tiny people fell to the ground. And a huge nanny, passing by, stooped, picked the Royal Edward from her colleague's woozy embrace and handed it to Nanny Destiny, who gave it to her bodyguard.

The Chief sat up. His head was in his hands.

A voice said, 'Be brave!' The voice of Nanny Destiny.

The Chief looked up.

'King Beowulf,' said Nanny Destiny.

'Vas?'

'Follow me,' she said. 'You know what we must do, ducksy wucksy ickle.'

'Do nicht talk to me zo. MEIN EDVARD!'

'Lemme put it another way. Do as you are told, or the bear gets it,' said Nanny Destiny.

The murmur of the crowd was becoming a grumble. The Nanas were closing up into a sort of squad. The air felt still and heavy and full of something invisible, the way it does before a thunderstorm.

'Lissen,' said Pete. 'What I think is, we better get you away from here.'

Reader, Daisy, Cassian and Primrose were tough folks. But they were in a hot city in Nananagua, stuck between vicious Nanas on one side and a mob on the other, with the sun beating down from the sky and the crunch of broken glass underfoot. At a time like this, even the toughest worry.

Though not necessarily about themselves.

'The poor Chief!' said Daisy.

'We must certainly go and fetch him,' said Primrose.

'Obviously,' said Cassian.

'Hur,' said a voice at their side. It was Giant Luggage. From the glint in his eye and the 3-metre stoker's shovel in his hand, it looked as if he felt the same way.

'Look out,' said Daisy. 'Something's happening.'

A nervous silence fell. The crowd watched uneasily.

A team of Nanas had uncovered the strange machine that had been on the articulated truck. As they stepped away, they revealed something huge and monstrous, squatting on the platform, gleaming in the Nananaguan sun.

The silence deepened.

It looked like a cannon with eight nozzles. A vast tank of water stood at its side. A thick power lead snaked back from it and in at a small door in the Great Hall. It had an unfriendly look. Almost as unfriendly as the squads of Nanas formed up on the steps and glaring into the square.

Correction. Unfriendlier. Much, much unfriendlier.

People started edging away from it.

'Forward to the rescue,' said Daisy.

15

The Darlings and their team shoved steadily through the crowd filling the square. In front of them, people jumped a short distance into the air, emitting squeaks of pain and outrage and looking down. From these signs Daisy deduced that Nosey Clanger was out there in the lead.

There was a crackle of loudspeakers. The voice of Nanny Destiny boomed over the square, thin but huge. 'People of Nananagua!' she cried in her cooing, hypnotic voice.

The people of Nananagua said, 'BOOOOO!'

'People of Nananagua,' fluted Nanny Destiny. 'How can you treat your old friend, the Nanny of the Nation, soooo? I have kept you safe –'

'By putting stupid warning labels on everything!' cried the crowd.

'And locking us up!' cried more of the crowd.

'Adjust bowler hats and up we go,' said Daisy.

'– and sound,' said Nanny Destiny, and now there was a steely edge to the flute, more like an alto sax really. 'But what I say now is, go to your homes!'

An avalanche of booing. 'We want Real Banana, the People's Friend!' shouted someone.

'Real Banana!' shouted the crowd like surf on a beach.

Down on the steps, the Nana squads stood firm, ready for anything. Up the steps between the squads came a group of people, three in nanny uniform, one very small, an eleven-year-old boy coated in engine oil, and a lumbering giant with a handle on the back of his head.

'Afternoon,' said the group politely.

'Afternoon,' grunted the Nana squads rudely. The Nana squads were not very polite to start off with, and now they were looking down at an enormous square full of angry people they were feeling even less polite than usual. And a bit . . . well, shaky, and wondering how things were at home. Not scared, exactly. Just . . . wishing they were somewhere else.

OK. Scared.

The Darlings and their escort nodded and smiled their way to the top of the steps, between the throne and the machine. The Chief was sitting on the steps of his throne, looking un-kingly. His crown was hanging over one of the knobs on the throne's back. His head was in his hands and he was talking to himself. Nanny Destiny walked over to him and kicked him sharply in the shin.

'Poor Chief,' said Daisy.

The Chief got up. His shoulders were bowed. He was looking at an enormous Nana. In one vast hand the Nana held the body of the Royal Edward. In the other she held its head. The head was still joined on to the body. But it was obvious that it would only take the smallest tweak of those great shoulders to –

Unthinkable.

Nanny Destiny said, from the side of her mouth, 'Turn on the jigsaw, King.'

The Chief stuck his tongue out at her and shook his head.

Nanny Destiny made a signal to the Nana holding the Royal Edward, who poked the bear in the stomach. 'GOOT EVENINK, YOUR ROYAL HIGHNESS,' said a tinny voice above the buzz and rumble of the crowd.

'NOOO!' cried the Chief, clutching his head. Shoulders bowed, head down, he shuffled towards the dreadful jigsaw. Or machine.

'Quick!' snapped Nanny Destiny at the Chief.

The Chief winced. Then, by chance, his eye caught Cassian's. Cassian winked. The Chief frowned. He paused. Then he straightened his shoulders and walked over to the machine.

Cassian stared at him, goggle-eyed.

The Chief had winked back.

'So,' said Nanny Destiny, stepping up to the microphone. Her voice boomed round the square. 'Your new King has made his Nana a jigsaw machine. And his Nana will use it. And you will not like it. Because these nozzles fire jets of water faster than fire-engine hoses. They will knock you over and roll you into the gutters. And the water contains a red dye, so that my faithful Nanas will know the troublemakers by their scarletness, and they will round up any who are left alive and fling them into the Caboose. Heh heh,' said Nanny Destiny, letting her true wickedness show.

'Ghastly woman,' said Daisy.

'King Beowulf I of Nananagua!' cried Nanny Destiny. 'Switch . . . ON!'

The Chief had been fiddling with the machinery. Now he grasped an enormous knife switch that stuck out of the jigsaw's left-hand side. He hauled it down. There was a great blue flash. Inside the machine's casing, pumps started to whine and wheels to churn. A quick, intense vibration came up through the flagstones under Daisy's feet.

'What does it do?' she said to Cassian.

'It's based on the Corby and Mazareene sludge pump, turbocharged and superheated,' hissed Cassian. 'With double –'

'Ssss,' said his sisters.

'You asked,' said Cassian, wounded.

'Very well!' said Nanny Destiny into the microphone. 'Ungrateful citizens, now you shall feel the power of my wrath!'

'She is going to shoot the crowd and lock them up,' said Daisy. 'And us too. Forever.'

'Oi,' said Pete, close to her ear. 'That nanny holdin' the Royal Edward. Look at her scars. It's Dangerfield! The Flying Nanny!'

Daisy looked. 'Goodness!' she cried. 'You're right! Luggage!'

Luggage had been staring at his feet, tittering a bit. Now he looked up, and his eyes focused on the nanny holding the bear. 'HUR!' he cried.

At the familiar and beloved sound, the nanny's head jerked round. Her tiny eyes met Luggage's tiny eyes. Her gigantic jaw fell open. Her arms dropped, until she was holding the bear by one leg only.

Daisy leaned towards Luggage. She said, 'Go to her, laddie!'

Luggage went.

'Look at Nanny Destiny!' hissed Primrose.

Nanny Destiny was climbing a small flight of steel steps on the back of the jigsaw. She swung herself into the padded operator's chair. She squinted down a set of sights at the crowd. Her little pink hands found pistol grips. Her fingers went to the triggers. Her black brogues went to the pedals.

'Luggage!' yelled Daisy. 'The bear!'

Luggage took the Royal Edward from his

beloved's limp fingers. He tossed the bear back over the heads of the crowd to Cassian. Cassian caught it neatly, changed hands, caught the Chief's eye and shouted, 'SWITCH OFF!'

The Chief shook his head, stuck out his enormous lower lip and put out his hands.

'Naughty Chief!' said Daisy.

'More interested in his silly bear than the welfare of thousands!' said Primrose.

'Give him the bear,' said Pete.

Cassian wound up and hurled the bear. The Chief's eyes grew big and round. He caught it easily, clasped it to his lardy bosom and sank to his knees, blubbering horribly.

'THE SWITCH!' roared the Darlings, Pete and Nosey.

'LIEBLING!' howled the Chief.

'THE SWITCH!'

'MEIN LOVADUCKABLOOBLUMBAAA-AAAAAAR!'

'Embarrassing, really,' said Primrose.

Nanny Destiny's lips curled into a cruel smile. Her knuckles whitened on the jigsaw's pistol grips. Her brogues danced on the pedals, swinging the awful machine on to the part of the crowd that contained the maximum number of mothers with prams, small children and ice-cream vans. 'VENGEANCE IS MINE!' she shrieked, savouring the moment.

'THE SW–' roared just about everyone.

Nanny Destiny squeezed the trigger of the jigsaw.

Daisy covered her eyes. There was an enormous whooshing noise, then a great, deep silence.

Daisy uncovered her eyes.

The crowd was still there. Everything was still there.

Except Nanny Destiny.

Where the operator's seat of the jigsaw had been was an empty space, from which rose a wisp of steam. Everyone in the crowd was looking up, heads tilted back as far as they would go.

Daisy followed their eyes.

High, high above and getting higher by the second was the jigsaw's seat, with Nanny Destiny in it. As Daisy watched, the seat fell away. Nanny Destiny soared on, one hand on her hat, the other thrust out in the Superman position, heading out to sea.

Someone started to clap.

Someone else joined in.

The clapping spread across the enormous square. Clutching the Royal Edward to his bosom, the Chief stood to attention and bowed, clicking his heels repeatedly. He said into the microphone, 'I haf much enjoyed my one half-hour as King of your extra nice country. A country too nice for this Destiny person, who is a thug, so I haf moved some pipes around and made other changes, with the results that you haf seen. Now I hand you over to your true presidente, Real Banana. And off ve go in my dear old *Kleptomanic*!'

'Hooraaaaaaaaaaaaaaaaaah!' roared the crowd.

Far out to sea, there was a medium-sized splash. Nobody paid any attention.

Except the sharks.

Steam hissed. A launch chugged. The brilliant white side of the *Kleptomanic* loomed overhead. A gangway came down. The Darlings, the Chief and their retinue strode up it and on to the bridge. The Captain made a signal. A steward, once a country-house butler and Inside Man, began sloshing Green Swizzle ingredients into a large glass jug.

'Ahem,' said Daisy.

Silence fell. Eyebrows rose.

'The time for celebration is not now,' said Daisy. 'Certainly Nanny Destiny has been prevented from stealing our lovely ship. But the key is apparently in the horrid drains of the House of the Beige Door, where it will never be found under any circumstances. It will be hard to replace. Till then, we are stuck here.'

'Manual override is indeed hardwired to an irrevocable systems meltdown with permanent and catastrophic ramifications,' said Cassian, who was certainly Papa Darling's son.

'Broken, then,' said Primrose.

Someone started sobbing.

Everyone looked round.

It was the Chief. He was holding the Royal Edward in front of him, staring into the boot-button eyes. 'Zo zorry, Edvard!' he spluttered through his tears. 'Zorry, zorry, but I must!'

'Must wha?' said Daisy, who was in no mood for exhibitions of this kind.

But the Chief had turned, and was sliding off the bridge and into the ship's interior.

Daisy, Cassian and Primrose followed.

The broad but twisted back led along

passageways and down companionways until it arrived deep, deep in the ship's middle. 'The sick bay,' said Cassian, pointing helpfully to a red cross on a door.

'And that,' said Primrose as the Chief pushed open the door opposite, 'is the operating theatre.'

In the theatre, the Chief was forcing himself into green surgical scrubs. He motioned to the Darlings to do likewise. It was folly to argue. Soon all were clad in green, with masks over their mouths and noses. The Chief's was wet, because he was still blubbing.

'Lights,' he sobbed.

Lights came on, glaring down on the operating table.

On which lay the Royal Edward.

'Anaesthetic,' said the Chief.

Primrose pulled the gas mask off its hook and strapped it to the bear's face.

The Chief held up a rubber-gloved hand. 'Schcalpel.'

Daisy placed a scalpel in his hand.

'I am goink in mit the number vun incision,' said the Chief. 'Mein Edvard!'

The scalpel came down. Cassian, who liked

machines but not tubing, felt sick. The Chief made a deep, confident cut in the bear's stomach. A wisp of sawdust curled into the lights followed by a small, dazed moth.

'Forceps!' cried the Chief.

Daisy placed the forceps in his hand.

The Chief probed delicately in the bear's interior, then withdrew the forceps. Gripped in the business end was a small but intricate golden key. 'Beholdt,' he said. He dropped the key into a kidney bowl Daisy held out, then burst into a storm of weeping.

'All right,' said Daisy, taking over. 'I shall close the incision with my busy needle. Cassian, you know what to do with the key. And Primrose, perhaps you might have something for the poor Chief in your wee larder?'

'A clear-cut case for Brighten-Up Bickies,' said Primrose.

Three minutes later, as the Chief was sucking horribly on a bicky and Daisy was putting in the last neat stitch, a delicate tremor came up through the operating-theatre floor.

'What's that?' said Primrose.

'Der Main Engine,' said the Chief, his eyes now bicky-dried.

'And here's your bear, good as new,' said Daisy.

'Edvard!' cried the Chief. 'Didda bad lady cut you up?'

'No, you did,' said Daisy, but of course he was not listening. 'Now I think we could go up to the bridge and be a bit triumphant.'

So there they were.

'Chief,' said the Captain, 'we must all thank you for the great sacrifice you made.'

'Do not thank me,' said the Chief. 'Thank Cassian.'

'Cassian wha?' said the astonished Primrose and Daisy, turning on their brother, who had gone deep red under his coating of oil.

'Ja. He took me up the wolkano to show me that Nenny Distaste –'

'Destiny.'

'– voteffer, told lies. End he reminded me of the kindness of all of you good thieves and burglars and childrens to me, how you found the Edvard, give me schips to mend, all that. So I stuffed the key into the Edvard through a bad seam – forgiff me, Edvard – or she vould have taken it and maybe cut off my head to get at it. Und here ve are.'

'Terribly kind of you,' said the Captain. 'Now then, Lars. We will all say our goodbyes, and then we will Make Ready for Sea!'

That night there were oxen roasted whole, obviously, plus fireworks and rather embarrassing folk dancing in front of the Great Hall of the People. Next morning, thousands lined Ciudad Olvidada's smelly quays as the *Kleptomanic*'s anchor came up, her siren blew a long blast, and she steamed out of the bay.

The crowds waved. The crew of the *Kleptomanic* waved back. Then, as the green mountains sank into the horizon, they went about their business. Papa Darling was scrubbing furiously at the lower-deck lavs – undignified yet strangely satisfying work, conducted far from the nearest rattlesnake. Giant Luggage had watched Nanny Dangerfield out of sight as she marched off with all the other Nanas to rebuild Nananagua's simply appalling roads. He was now doing a little sentimental work on the Heavy Bag in the ship's gym. Sophie Nickit was standing back from her Advanced Pickpocketing class, whose trousers were falling round its ankles.

And the Darlings?

Silly question, really. Obviously Primrose was in the galley, supervising the icing of a replica of El Volcano Grande that unlike the original erupted large volumes of raspberry lava. Cassian was in the engine room, regreasing number-five thrust bearing and wondering in a dazed way whether he had done his clever and bendy thing with the Chief's mind on purpose (the Captain's version) or by accident (his own version). Pete Fryer was on the bridge, reading the verse of Larson E. Profitt the Burglar Poet to the Captain, who listened with a Green Swizzle in one hand and her eyes far away. And Daisy was playing chess with Nosey Clanger.

'Look!' said Nosey. 'A flying nanny!'

'Last time you said that you were trying to cheat,' said Daisy. 'Not this time.' She moved her bishop. 'Checkmate.'

And on sailed the *Kleptomanic*, past a solitary brown bowler hat bobbing on the waves, towards Palmbeachia, holiday paradise of the western seas, and the far blue waters beyond.